Shungu

THE BULL TERRIER

IVY HOVE

WORKBOOK PRESS LLC
187 E Warm Springs Rd,
Suite B285, Las Vegas, NV 89119, USA

Website:	https://workbookpress.com/
Hotline:	1-888-818-4856
Email:	admin@workbookpress.com

Ordering Information:
Quantity sales. Special discounts are available on quantity purchases by corporations, associations, and others.
For details, contact the publisher at the address above.

Library of Congress Control Number:
ISBN-13:   978-1-955459-93-8 (Paperback Version)
              978-1-955459-94-5 (Digital Version)

REV. DATE: 15/06/2021

Shungu the Bull Terrier

A Story by the dog Shungu

Ivy Hove

Dedication

To my dogs Shungu, Shumba,
Sheba, Tonga and Terry

Acknowledgements

I am hugely indebted to my late mother-in-law for encouraging my husband and I to entrust the security of our home and our lives to the tried animal friends. Without the dogs, Shungu would never have existed as part of our family history and this book would never have been written.

I thank my loving children for reminiscing with me on our earlier family life with our dogs all those years ago.

I also want to thank all the people who inspired me to put pen to paper at last after putting off the actual writing of this book for so long.

Lastly, and by no means the least, my thanks go to the Birmingham Libraries at Sutton Coldfield Shopping Centre, King Standing Circle and Perry Common. The library staff went to great lengths to attend to the library users' needs.

Contents

Dog's Prayer

O Lord of all creatures, grant that man, my master, may be as faithful to other men as

I am to him.

Make him as loving towards his family and friends, as I am loving to him.

Grant that he may guard with honesty the good things with which

Thou has endowed him as honestly as I guard his.

Give him, O Lord, a happy and ready smile,

as happy and spontaneous as the wagging of my tail.

Make him as ready to show gratitude as I am eager to lick his hand.

Give him patience as great as mine

as I await his return without complaining. Grant him my courage and my readiness to

sacrifice all for him, even my life. May he possess my youthful spirit and joy of thought.

O Lord of all creatures, as I am in truth only a dog, may my master always be truly a man

Pero Scanziani

Foreword

When my late mother-in-law suggested we adopt a watchdog, I absent-mindedly assented out of my respect for her without even giving her proposal a thought. She was on her first visit with us from my husband's rural home since our return from the diaspora in 1980 to an independent Zimbabwe. We had just rented a four-bedroomed house in a low- density suburb along a main road, not very far from the Harare town centre. While I busied myself making our new home comfortable, my mother-in-law had managed to gather intelligence on the security situation in the city in general, and the low-density suburbs in particular. The intelligence, though anecdotal, was as startling as it was disturbing. Indeed, crime rates could have been lower in some parts of any area for certain items, certain areas being easily accessible whether high or low density.

Though I realised something had to be done about matters of home security, at that time the subject had to be shelved as there was so much to do already. But reports of newly committed crimes in all urban and rural areas continued to reach us through the media or even first-hand via our neighbours.

With the scrapping of discrimination in the laws of Zimbabwe that year, the country was going through rapid and radical changes in all spheres of life. There was greater access to better housing, employment, goods and services, most of which had long been the preserve of the white population of the country during the pre-independent era. In eager leaps and bounds, after independence, the majority of the African people at every social level availed themselves to the many opening opportunities to improve their life chances. Many attained their aspirations or were well set on the course to achieve them. However, there were many more rural and city dwellers trapped in the vicious cycle of poverty and who continued the struggle to make a living through honest means and resourcefulness. But there were also many others who had long sunk into a life of crime due to lack of opportunities for the majority of Africans in the pre-independence era and who had little, if any, hope of reforming. In this category would be found opportunistic thieves, young and adult experienced wheelers and dealers working individually or in groups to feed families. A good number in this category were also obsessed with the desire to possess symbols of success like prestigious cars and household and garden gadgets, not to mention spending amounts of cash far beyond their reach through legal means.

The idea of home and family security having taken root, I soon found myself making a double take whenever I spotted a high walled and gated house, or professionally guarded ones as I drove to and from work or visiting relations. Without doubt, it would have been illusory on my part to even think it was within our stretched finances, at that stage in our life settling back home, to emulate such costly security measures. In the following few weeks my head grew increasingly obsessed with thoughts of dogs. A watchdog seemed to be the reasonable and, indeed, affordable answer to secure some degree of safety for our home. With some anxiety, I soon started combing "The Herald" advertisements for a dog. With my pretty scanty or, more precisely, to no knowledge about dogs at that stage, coupled with the feeling of urgency to protect our homestead and the family, I convinced myself that any dog was welcome. When I brought the black slick furred puppy home, he bounded up a few steps to the low open veranda at the front of the house. Without hesitation, he cuddled up with my mother-in-law who sighed with relief as she smilingly stroked Shungu. That was how my family started the life-long journey with Shungu and other dogs which came and fell on the wayside, learning to appreciate and respect each other as different species of creation.

As for me there were no regrets over the 17 years throughout which Shungu, as a watchdog, protected us and our home.

Introduction

Shungu was an exceptional dog with an active intelligence, in some respects, almost human. He was decidedly loyal and affectionate to the human family members of the pack including children and puppies. Like any Staffordshire bull terrier, he was brave, robust and fierce, especially through his insistent, sharp bark. But Shungu could also be quite a terror sometimes, particularly when defending his territory against animal or human intrusion much to the family's embarrassment.

My son, Sean in the story, summed up Shungu perfectly. He explained, "On the surface, Shungu looks like any ordinary, feisty dog. But a few minutes with him will reveal he has a 'personality' setting him apart from other dogs as demonstrated by the pattern of some of his actions and calculated behaviour as a guard dog." There was also something exciting and interesting about his presence which made it an immense pleasure to have him as a family pet. He seemed to command more attention than most of our dogs, just by his lively energy and other endearing traits.

Much of this book, though largely fictitious, is based on some true incidents of Shungu's feats of excellence as a guard dog protecting the property and members of his family pack.

All human names are fictitious. Except for Tessa, the dogs featured in the book existed as such. I never came to know the name of the cat. The name Whisky belonged to the cat of the two lovely sisters, both in their nineties, who were our next door neighbours in London in the seventies. Whisky was adored by our very young children then.

Chapter One

My name is Shungu. I'm a dog and member of a family resident in a low-density suburb of Harare. Having been a watchdog all my life, I have become a stickler about security revealing only scanty identifying particulars. My family now lives in a huge house standing bang in the middle of a large property on the outskirts of the metropolitan city. I have come to know that dogs, like all breathing things, have their last day here on earth. By that I mean they die; life comes to an end. Well, I feel that during my life with this family I have been a good dog.

I have not been a lazy, slobbering lay about with no sense of commitment to duty. I have been a loving dog as far as the word can be applied to dogs. I have tried to execute my duties well and sometimes too well that I exceeded the mark. You see, I would like the world to know how loyal I have been or the likes of us can be. How else have we earned the honour of being called man's best friend! So that is why I now write my memoirs before it is too late and there-in lay out my experiences: good and bad contributions to the life of the family and how I have achieved these.

I do not remember when I was born or what happened to my dog family. By this I mean my dog mum and dad or even my dog brothers and sisters for that matter. Dogs, like humans, share that origin, don't they? I do have a hazy recollection of my human mum lifting me from her car and pouring some milk in a bowl for me which I lapped up shamefully quickly, not so much to allay a burning thirst as to indulge my taste buds. Well, not a brilliant idea as my tummy did not take to the stuff. The young man who met mum at the gate of the breeder's home had made it a quick transaction.

There had been no handover briefing regarding what breed I was, the vaccinations I had received or my diet. He pocketed the money that mum had handed over to him, politely explained that he was in some kind of a hurry and zoomed away on his motor bike. The gardener closed the gate behind mum and I, shaking his head in silence.

During my first week or two, I shared the main house with my human family. After my first fill of milk, I had started belching repeatedly then after a little while, heaven broke loose! Of course I didn't even know what was happening to me, but I was terrified. The visiting granny, the cook and mum on her return from work, all had a hectic time cleaning the floor and washing hands! Somehow, in my naivety it became apparent that I was the cause of the drama. Mum put a small bowl of water near me which I took no notice of at first. A little later she took me out for my first walk in the homestead yard, along the waist-high hedge which I found exhilarating as I skipped and trotted behind her.

After she shovelled loose soil on my mess to block away the inevitable swarms of flies that entered the house. I realised I had recovered somewhat and the bloated feeling had abated. She then put another bowl of raw meat before me to which I applied myself cautiously coming back to the bowl after some rest. Things went well this time round and from then on it was a balanced diet of solids, home cooked food, dog meats and fortified dog cereals from the supermarket.

The human family had recently settled in this suburb not too far from the great city centre. They had just returned from the diaspora to a new Zimbabwe.

There was so much excitement and jubilant talk about the new life with the words 'freedom' 'independence' 'the ruling party' popping everywhere in conversations even when visitors drove by. There seemed to be not much else in human talk those early days in my life. Such euphoria!

The Mabvira family consisted of mum Wendy, father Daniel and their three children, Kate, Sean and Thembi. I couldn't have been blessed with a more caring family and being a fledgling and blundering puppy, my capacity to reciprocate was somewhat limited in those days. I could only frisk about to express my appreciation, yapping and licking anyone attending to me with my tiny tongue. Back then I was allowed in at night time after the whole day roaming outside in our yard. In good time a solid typical dog kennel was procured and made comfortable for me. It soon became a pleasure to curl up to sleep in my kennel basket.

In the beginning, I never thought I would ever settle out there but I quickly got used to the freedom and cool early morning breeze. Of course, I didn't appreciate in those early days that my family had opened their home for me to fulfil a watchdog function and naturally to be able to do that, I had to be outside the house trotting about in the homestead yard and sleeping there for the night with my ears pricked up for unusual sounds!

For a long while, I had ignored the barking of the other bigger dogs in the neighbourhood which could be irritatingly loud, though not as persistent and in my view, threatening as the ones next door to the right of our homestead.

At night the noise was so loud and ferocious that my little body shivered with fright even though it was warm and comfortable in the kennel. Somehow, despite it all, I managed to get some sleep. In this life of mine, I could not work out how many of those dogs there were next door, as they sometimes thundered down towards the road that also passed our yard. It sounded as though there were hundreds of them. Sometimes it seemed they were making for my open kennel.

But by now, almost a year later, I had confirmed that the yard next door was securely walled and gated. But the barking, growling and trudging by these dogs next door still reduced me to a whimpering and shaking wreck. The same could not be said about the yard of our rented house which had a wall, a hedge dotted with yawning gaps and an un-gated driveway. One day I forgot my fears and strolled out of our yard and through a tiny gap I detected those dogs next door. I beat a retreat but I had been spotted. The two full grown hounds tore down to their closed gate like wolves after a deer, barking so madly and baring their sharp teeth as if to munch open the gate. As I entered the security of my hut I swore never to be so damn stupid again as to venture near the hounds' gate.

I was growing fast and getting to know much more about our yard and the dog community in the neighbourhood. I also began to be more and more aware of the much talked about burglaries sweeping most low-density households, whether guarded by dog or not. Only a sprinkling of families in the neighbourhood could afford the services of professional guards from registered companies.

I did not see the hounds for a long time but they will never know how their barking, growls and loud brawling sometimes sent me cringing into a corner of my kennel in the dark of night. They appeared in my dreams and gave me a turn one night after another visit to the vet for a jab and a dip. That night I struggled to settle down. For starters I was still hurting from the vaccination for protection against certain diseases including rabies and some others that I cannot remember. Second, there was serious barking from the immediate and far reaches of the neighbourhood, on a night that I was sensitive to every noise.

As for the fellows next door, they seemed to be responding to the call of every dog near or far. Sleep continued to be as elusive as a crook on the run and so I took a few safe walks here and there. When I had crossed over the road, with much trepidation, I gave my howled responses with all the strength I could muster.

It so happened, I could not remember actually getting back into the kennel. But suddenly, it seemed the hounds next door had jumped over their walled garden onto the road outside, barking fiercely and making straight for my kennel. Then as I scampered out to flee, I jumped over what turned out to be the vet's concrete treatment table.

I looked back and the hounds had transformed into a huge black crow swooping down to jab its beak right onto the spot of my injection. I howled with pain, excruciating and gripping pain, deep in my flesh. I moaned loudly but then realised, as I woke up, that I was right here in my kennel. Where had those animals vanished to - the hounds, the black winged beast? It was then that it dawned on me that I had a horrible nightmare, and what a bloody nightmare it was!

What a relief it was to know with certainty that there had never been such a horror threatening my life in reality. With a sigh I performed a jig on my two hind feet yapping happily. There was no one to share my absolute joy and celebration with. It was still just after dawn, the morning air nice and cool, and the time the guards at the eighth house on this road went off duty. By now I no longer felt the discomfort of that dreadful injection.

I had grown to be comfortable in my immediate environment and my curiosity tempted me to venture out further from familiar grounds. One mid-morning, without any resistance, I cantered down to the small but well patronized shopping centre down the road in the neighbourhood. I could not believe what I had come upon as I turned a corner and the place burst into full view. I had never thought the world had this much to offer! There before me stretched an array of different shops specialising in all sorts of retail items: a supermarket for groceries and sundries, a bookshop, and a florist with an explosion of her colourful merchandise on display. There was the aroma of strong coffee from an espresso bar. Next to an ice-cream parlour stood a fish and chips outlet. The smell of the french-fries was overpowering and I started drooling as I crept into the shop. Of course, I was ordered to "get out" with an accompanying string of not-so-nice invectives. My shaking tail now between my legs, I scampered far out to the edges of the shopping centre grounds.

There was no smell of food at all coming from a big black bin stationed there. I later learned that the bins began to fill with left overs at lunch time. I always had good lunch at home and so I waited till after my afternoon snooze. I made for the shopping centre again early in the evening. As I made for the bin, now on its side I could see in the dim light several dogs feasting there. I moved to join in and a huge Alsatian fixed a threatening gaze on me and gave a long threatening growl. It was made plain I was not welcome at that joint, but I stood my ground. As the Alsatian resumed scavenging, I threw myself on to the mixed mess of food which had been pulled out of the bin onto the ground.

I could not believe how fast I succeeded to claim a goodly share and more so, when one by one the satiated members of the pack started to walk away. I trotted halfway home with one dog that was a little bit older than I was and noticed he entered a yard a few houses down to the left of ours.

One afternoon mum and dad had gone to see how the renovations at the new house they had bought were progressing. I had followed the car and got wandering further than I normally did. Somehow there was something disturbing about the oblong building ahead, at a fork junction. I stopped in my tracks to give this building a good look-over. The feeling of déjà vu came over me. Then I saw the vet's dipping tub outside the dull looking surgery,

"The vet!" I exclaimed in recognition and utter disbelief.

"Oh well, got to get back home at once."

I turned and ran as fast as my little strong feet could carry me. Then unexpectedly I sighted that shopping centre again. I made straight for the bin, but then remembering the discomfort I felt in my stomach after the last scavenging adventure, I decided to continue on home. I did not get far before I fell in with my friends Boki and his mother, Rona. We had first met on my earlier visit, when I discovered the shopping centre and we have roamed the neighbourhood together ever since. Thinking I was heading for the shops, Rona warned me not to bother.

"There's nothing interesting in the bin yet. Let's go home, Boki." Boki slacked behind with me chatting sweet nothings as we trotted along together in amity. Just as I remembered what I really wanted to ask him ever since we met, his human mum called him and he trotted off.

Chapter Two

A Miss as Good as a Mile

I had been carousing around the eastern side of our yard just before midnight when I sniffed what I had become to know as the human scent. Just as the strangeness of the sweaty odour hit me I detected a human form lurking around Sean's bicycle which was parked in the veranda. I stopped in my tracks to make absolutely sure the person now wheeling the bicycle was not family. I went berserk, barking like mad as I fell upon the intruder.

Dad peered through the window from upstairs to see what was going on. He must have seen me by the dim street light tugging at the trousers of an intruder who by now had dropped the bicycle. The intruder slipped and jumped the hedge bordering the eastern side of the house. By this time dad had already reached the ground floor on his way to help. I had ignored dad's call for me to come back as he bounced down the steps outside the kitchen. It was too late as everything happened very fast.

The hedge was not too high for me to scale and get the thief but by the time I landed on the other side, I had momentarily lost his scent. I stood there non-pulsed but still barking my heart out, trying to figure out which direction the elusive thief had run. Just then a ramshackle truck parked in the distance by the roadside took off and sped towards town with a rough grating sound. Just as he shot out of the kitchen door, Dad had caught a blurred view of the intruder striding towards the hedge. He had also heard the thudding steps of someone on the run. He tried to read the registration number of the get-away truck but failed to do so.

I pursued the truck for a short distance while dad called me back. In a state of frustrated agitation, I jumped over the hedge back into our yard. Dad had picked the bicycle up and so I followed him as he wheeled it into the kitchen. I could tell he was aware of what had nearly happened and that I acted quickly to save Sean's treasured toy. He instructed me to sit and patting my back he repeatedly said, 'good boy.' His joy was palpable and I felt good inside.

The gardener had slept in his cabin throughout the incident and was surprised to hear what he had missed when dad told him. All the gardener said was, "Oh, bicycles are a popular target for thieves in these suburbs," and went about his morning routine.

I had never seen Sean so happy as he strode toward me in the morning. He spent more time with me than usual that day and it seemed as if right then, nothing mattered to him more than I did. He knelt on the lawn and embraced my dog face as he radiated utter joy, gratitude and respect. I felt warm inside. What a way to start a day!

It's only when I opened my eyes mid-morning that I realised I must have dropped into an exhausted sleep as soon as I curled up on my cushioned dog house floor. I was not in the habit of taking frequent snoozes. Soon enough, I was already trotting about all over our yard when I remembered the harrowing event of the night before.

Chapter Three

Beloved Doba

Quite a few unfortunate events were reported in suburbs and neighbourhoods but nothing surpassed theft and burglary and the speed at which the news was sensationalised and spread among residents. Gardeners, child-minders and cooks would vie for the house telephone to share the news with friends across suburbia. The impact on persons contemplating or intent on such heinous mischief was not insignificant whenever a ferocious dog featured in frustrating what they would consider a happy outcome. Property owners, on hearing my acts of heroism envied my mum and dad for owning such a vigilant and active dog. Soon after another stellar watchdog performance, mum took me for a walk on a lead.

As we passed the house few gates down from ours, the lady owner, Mrs Peterson, who was driving through the gate, stopped her car and chatted with mum whilst pointing at me through the car window. Looking me over the lady said,

"That must be Shungu!"

Mrs Peterson started comparing me with her dog. Eyes rolling benignly, she confided in mum. "Our family dog is so laid back it seems he actually takes the thieves round the house to show them the best things to steal." Mum almost doubled over with laughter but I couldn't join her as being a dog, nature denied us that physical capacity. Between chokes of laughter mum called out,

"What's your dog's name?"

The dog revealed itself as it walked towards the gate, stopped to gaze at us lethargically, before it made a U-turn in silence and disappeared to the backyard.

"We named him Doba meaning 'catch,' as a puppy. Of course, we were not thinking of that breed called Doberman because as you can see he isn't. He is a Dane in midlife," said Mrs Peterson.

"It seems there are so many breeds of dogs," observed mum.

"Oh, yes. Talking about this one, we thought he would at least bark to stave away the thieves. He certainly decided not to live up to his name."

"But you seem to be managing well," suggested mum.

"Managing well? No. We experienced a nasty break-in beginning of the year."

"You don't say," mused mum.

Oh yes, my new colour television and beer cooler disappeared. There was a round cutting on one of our lounge window panes, large enough for the hand of a fully-grown man to get through and open the window wider. Doba didn't even bother to bark and warn us. Currently we are looking for a professional night guard. We do hear Shungu barking fiercely sometimes. You were lucky there!" Mrs Peterson said

"Why do you say so?" Mum asked.

"It takes desperately brave crooks to brave a place watched by a dog like Shungu. His barking is getting stronger and not easy for many thieves to ignore," said Mrs Peterson, starting her car to drive into her yard. Then she popped her head out of the window to keep mum's attention. "But in spite of everything we do love Doba dearly. He is absolutely adorable and so friendly," Mrs Peterson enthused, fondly watching Doba while pushing back a stubborn strand of her blond hair.

"I would have thought so. See you later," assented mum and

smiling benignly we proceeded on our walk.

Some months passed. Then one day, driving home from work mum saw Mrs, Peterson outside her gate and stopped to inquire how she was getting on with her search for a security guard.

"We're still considering what would be the best option. You see, we have to be careful which professional security companies to approach."

"I thought all security companies adhered to uniform professional standards of work and gave their candidates special training before they were ready for hire, don't they?" mum offered.

"That's true, but it's the quality of the training that's important, is it not?" cut in Mrs Peterson.

"It looks like some of the security companies mushrooming everywhere these days are often impatient for quick earnings and consequently, do not do a thorough job of it sometimes. One has to be pretty cautious about these things in these times."

"How have you come to that conclusion? Surely the company managers should be aware that it's counter-productive to rush things through," mum observed.

"Aware or not, there have been happenings, according to the grapevine, indicating the performance and integrity of security guards from some of these companies leaves a lot to be desired. Take for instance the incident reported to have happened at a house two blocks down. The shoe prints of a night security guard were stamped all around the bare floor of a makeshift shed over which was suspended two huge bunches of yellowing bananas. Not a single banana had been spared. The family had brought the fruits from their village home in Honde Valley after a relaxing weekend there. On assuming duty the following evening, the same guard was taken to the shed from where the bananas had been stolen. His shoe prints matched those found on the floor by the dad of the family. The guard confessed and asked for forgiveness but there was no mercy because the family could no longer trust him. A substitute was brought from another company. This was no isolated episode. Acts of such gross misconduct by security

guards had at some point been sensationalised by the media prompting publication of newspaper articles headed

"Who will Guard the Guards?" concluded Mrs Peterson. She went on,

"I remember scanning past such a title in a Sunday paper editorial some months ago. I skipped the article, not knowing that one day I would have such a keen interest on the subject of household and family security."

"Oh! How ironic. I'm sure you'll find a reliable guard soon. I must get home now, it's been a long day," mum said and drove home confident that Mrs. Peterson's security issue would definitely be sorted someday soon.

Chapter Four

An Inside Job

It transpired that one weekend, several months after the failed attempt to steal Sean's bicycle, my human family visited their rural home. On their return the bicycle was nowhere to be found. Sean really wanted to take his bike on the visit with him. However, the truck had a functional problem and the sedan boot was full of grocery and luggage. On their return, on the Sunday afternoon, the first thing Sean was dying to do after greeting me was ride his bicycle.

"Hey people, I can't believe this! My bicycle seems to have disappeared," announced Sean, his body language suggestive of having received a jab of torture. Mum was tired and her head must have been reeling with Monday morning work plans. "Sean, go and look properly. Where did you leave it? I hope not in the veranda again," Mum tried to speak but Sean cut her short.

"It's gone. It's not there! Mum, dad!" Sean shouted in a panic.

"You're supposed to help here," mum reminded him.

"Hey Sean. Go and help mum to take things out of the car before you go riding," ordered dad firmly, tugging a hold of all his and mum's things upstairs. When everything was packed properly from the car boot, Sean searched thoroughly for the bike without success.

"My bicycle is gone!" He shouted for all to hear and started to cry. By this time, I was puzzled about what was troubling Sean.

"It's the bicycle. I don't see it anywhere."

I soon figured it out. There was no ignoring Sean anymore. Everyone in the family was geared up into overdrive and joined the search including dad, albeit briefly. There weren't many places the bicycle could have been. Denial had taken an unusual hold on us all. The same places were searched several times over. Desperation led to such ridiculous antics some of which assumed comic proportions. I tried to register my support by frantically dashing inside and outside the house barking like mad wishing Sean's bike to materialise. What could have happened to it? Did that intruder return with more honed up tactics to make a success of it this time around?

By this time, Sean had locked himself in his bedroom. I knew he was very upset and could hear him crying. I had failed him but I was still assured of his friendship and love. Of that I was convinced based on past experience. I also knew the time would come soon when Sean would approach me and share. But still in anguished silence I agonised over my failure to protect the bike.

The family had always welcomed relatives in their home. Most of them came for one service or another to which they had limited access in the rural communities. At that time, we had mum's half-brother, Kane, a funny but brilliant chap who had joined the family to be able to further his education at Species College in town. He had been with us now for two terms. There was also dad's cousin who had long finished school. However, so far she had been unable to secure a job.

Since the mysterious disappearance of the bike my trust in humanity had plummeted a great deal. I found myself suspicious of anyone outside of the family, visiting relatives. I started growling at the gardener and Kane. The sight of dad's relation removing the washing from the line outside began disturbing me. Of course, I began to regard everybody except my human family members with suspicion. Indeed, why would I not consider the possibility of the current boarding relations colluding to spirit away the bike, I speculated. But somehow, I knew the family would not approve if I behaved badly – something I would have loved to do in my present vexed mood of mounting suspicion.

I had no doubt mum and dad would have by now obtained on accounts on the whereabouts of these guest relatives from Friday mid-day when the family drove away to their arrival back late Sunday afternoon. Apart from that fact, my observation of how the two relatives interacted had confirmed my opinion that there was no blood lost between them. They did not trust each other enough, it seemed, to become accomplices in crime. The gardener, VaJairos had taken his usual weekend off mid-morning on Saturday to show up back for his duties Monday morning. There was no way he could have whisked the bicycle away as I was hovering around the yard most of the time to welcome back the absent family any time.

Kane had long covered for VaJairos in the business of preparing food for me in his absence. I eyed him with unconcealed disapproval each time he dished my food. He already had an annoying tendency to give me too much and I was not a glutton by any measure. Obviously, the crash coaching by VaJairos had not been quite adequate because the young man was a 'B' pupil according to his secondary school grades. It could be that he just was blasé about proper portions when preparing my food or that of any of the other household pets for that matter.

It's quite probable he had been under the impression that the gardener was skimping on the portions when giving me food and had all along been aspiring to right what he viewed as a wrong. Anyway, I just took my fill and left the rest inwardly wondering what he took me for- an elephant?

With short notice, dad's brother and his young family of four- Joshua and Margret, a boy of 11years and a younger girl -had returned home to Zimbabwe from England. Naturally, the family lodged with us while searching for a home of their own. There was no way dad was going to let his brother and family go homeless while the two families could share what space was available at our address. It seemed to me in Zimbabwe, that the tradition of sharing basic conveniences was a value far deeply ingrained and too compelling to ignore.

The double-story house which my family rented had four double bedrooms, a large balcony upstairs and a veranda downstairs.

During the first two nights, the children of the two families camped in the upstairs balcony and so they pulled mattresses from their bedrooms onto the reed mats spread carefully on the floor. The noise was intolerable- screaming, shouting cat-fights, periodic bulletins and reports from the younger ones - the lot! On the third day, dad ordered the mattresses to be returned to their beds and firmly forbade any more noise because people needed to sleep well to cope with work the following day.

Due to the expanded household mum asked the gardener to sound out whether his friend who had been released next door was interested in two days paid work a week, helping with laundry. I had seen VaPeter when he was a cook next door for the white settlers who recently left the country for good. He often visited VaJairos for a chat in his cabin and, sometimes, they went out together after hours returning home almost at midnight.

Dad's cousin had left a week before his brother's family took residence with us. It seemed to me that the bike theft incident had been forgotten by the family but it still haunted me for a long time. Sometimes I dreamt about Kane whisking the bike away or sometimes dad's cousin handing it to a friend of hers over the waist-high hedge at the back of the yard. Then I would remind myself dreams were as good as conjecture with no proof. They constituted no reliable basis to accuse anybody for such a serious crime. I would then wonder what on earth had happened to that bike. On those occasions; I worked myself into utter misery. Huffing with consuming anger I would gaze into the distance wondering how the thief had so completely eluded me. For I never left the premises at night as that was the time most burglaries occurred.

Dad's brother had now bought a house and would be moving out with his family as soon as it was practical to do so. But to pack up their possessions, Margret persuaded VaPeter to do a few extra days starting the following morning to which he had agreed.

It was a hectic morning and the pressure was mounting. The situation was made more intense because Joshua and Margret were reporting for work in their respective professions in the next few days. They would be back home around five o'clock in the evenings.

To begin with VaPeter and VaJairos were cracking jokes as they forged on with their respective tasks. It had been my observation through experience that VaPeter sometimes took orders from his workmate who tended to be a bit bossy. I suspected he resented it but chose to remain shtum about it. On this hectic morning, his patience ran out and he snapped. There was no way of anyone predicting the conflagration that suddenly erupted before us. Suddenly all hell broke loose! They started shouting at each other. The altercation was conducted in a Malawian dialect; many years previously both had emigrated from the neighbouring country as teenagers to the green pastures of what was then known as Southern Rhodesia.

Mum was in the kitchen preparing lunch. She wondered if these long-time thick friends were really quarrelling as her knowledge of the language was minimal. It was fortunate that Margret's relative, conversant with a few Malawian dialects had come by to help her. Both were busy upstairs when they dashed down the stairs asking if mum was alright.

"I do understand their language, they are having a serious tiff threatening each other," announced the lady visitor called Bertha. She went on, "VaPeter is saying something about reporting VaJairos." At that point mum opened the door and called, "VaJairos what seems to be the matter? Why are you at each other's throats?" she asked. Bertha, straining for the appropriate words, demanded to know what VaPeter was now dying to report. She repeated the question with a firm insistence locking eyes with VaPeter's. The latter cleared his throat and after a pause during which VaJairos, shaking uneasily and trying to steady himself said,

"The bicycle."

Mum asked, "What bicycle? Why report about a bicycle? Who has got a bicycle here?"

"Come out with it VaPeter. Tell us, we haven't got all day," Bertha urged.

"Sean's bicycle -VaJairos stole it and left it with me, in my cabin next door to look after. He long took it back and I have no idea where it is now," revealed VaPeter. VaJairos had tried in vain to stop VaPeter from spilling the beans. But by then the cat was already out of the bag glaring at VaJairos!

Mum was aghast, "VaJairos, did you steal the bicycle?" she asked in a lowered, controlled voice. She was now seething with emotion and disbelief. VaJairos looked utterly shattered as he admitted responsibility for the incident.

There had never been any love lost between me and VaJairos but he was the last person I suspected. I had seen Sean pushing the bike into the house where he obediently left it over that fateful weekend.

Mum asked VaJairos if he would like to tell her how he accomplished the bike theft with people around. She explained that the family needed to identify loopholes and fix them to tighten security around and in the home. rather long perplexed pause she turned to VaJairos and asked,

"Where was Shungu?"

"I did it in stages. When everyone including Shungu was seeing you off that weekend you all went home, I entered the kitchen and deftly took the bike out. I quickly secreted it in my cabin and then on Saturday while Shungu was having his meal, I dropped the bike in the alleyway over the hedge. I then went round to wheel the bike through the wicket gate into Peter's cabin. I sold it. I'm sorry, Amai."

When Sean heard how the theft was conducted he emitted a huge sigh and exclaimed, "Indeed, it was an inside job. VaJairos, tell me, did you have anything to do with the failed attempt to steal my bike, the other time Shungu rescued it?" Sean asked. "Oh, no it wasn't me at all," replied VaJairos. "So how are we to trust what you say now? Yes, it was you or your friends," Mum insisted.

"No mum. Maybe that's where I got the idea from but it wasn't me that time. I'm not a thief. All my life I never stole anything. It was the devil that tempted me mum. Please, forgive me," VaJairos was shattered. At that moment VaPeter was still unaware of the full implication of his role in the eyes of the law.

Both VaJairos and VaPeter lost their jobs and received a caution from the police covering the suburb-the former for theft and the later for accepting and receiving stolen property. Dad didn't want to sue but still paid the culprits for the work done in the family home up to that month. He had dispensed the dismissal through the police. At that time arbitrary termination of employment for all workers had been outlawed under the new government of the country to guard against discrimination.

Chapter Five

The Big Move

There had been talk of moving to a better house for some months now. It all had little meaning to me. The following days were full of events which absorbed me so completely I had scarcely any time to remember neither the dreams nor nightmares of the previous nights. The next-door hounds seemed to have been taken to dog kennels and were no longer my torment. Their family had taken the popular route down south and soon another family had taken over the mansion. As for our abode, there was no way the homestead would be walled and gated by mum and dad because the property was rented.

And so I busied myself trotting round the big house ensuring its security. You see, it had been my observation this time that humans in general feared venturing into yards with dogs reputed for their ferocity and I was getting known in the suburb as growing to be such a dog. I also liked to try my uncertain powers over passers-bye who reacted to my barking with a great show of fright. Through the gaps in the hedge, I would catch sight of pedestrians passing by. I would deliberately exaggerate my fury towards those who had a hesitancy and uncertainty about them and those who might be contemplating coming into our yard. I refrained from biting anyone primarily due to fear of being hurt back but I would in time outgrow this fear as I became more courageous.

Sometimes I would trot out of our yard and roam a bit farther towards the shopping centre just for the kicks. For some time, I had not been in touch with Rona and Boki. I had stopped trawling bins for food because I had experienced several bouts of extreme tummy discomfort after each episode. Besides, there was no great need for that, as I was well fed, loved and appreciated by my family. Mum and the children took me on a lead for long walks along the pavements and, on a few occasions, to some well-manicured garden parks.

Dad liked to pat and watch me enjoy bones which he brought home especially for me. I looked forward to the quality time with dad, which stretched a bit longer from the time the penny dropped that I should restrain myself from jumping all over him and leaving smudges on his work suits. That was after I started to respond aptly to the instructions 'sit,' 'stay' and a few others which took quite a while to grasp as I puzzled over to understand what the fuss was all about!

So I had settled nicely into this cosy life when, one Saturday mid-morning, I caught sight of a colossal removal van reversing into our yard. I swooped down to investigate. I barked so fiercely running up and down the length of the van and even venturing to bite the wheels ignoring mum's attempts to calm me down.

"What! ...A moving house?! It's going to smash into ours. Oh!" I panicked. The van driver, a hunk of a man with a handsome, sweaty full face remained seated, cowering behind the steering wheel long after stopping the vehicle.

I had worked myself up into such a frenzy that even after dad secured me to a guava tree by using my lead, I continued straining to free myself completely overwhelmed with fury. After dad and the gardener had managed to heave my dog house into the Land Rover and started off, I followed with the children in mum's car. At last, the long awaited move to the new house had been accomplished with minimum hustle and bustle, at least from the way I saw things. The evening found me pacing the vast yard in the middle of which a huge, magnificent house proudly sprawled.

So many trees! Fully-grown weeping willows stood like sentinels fifty yards from the veranda of the dwelling house. There were three of these willow trees with their cascades shading a variety of flowers including white and yellow lilies and fuchsias. An open-mouthed fish gargoyle was perched on a dry fountain as if parched and pleading for drinking water. Making their own statement were a profusion of perennial fuchsias enjoying the cool shade of other nameless trees which seemed to have been growing for hundreds of years.

The ubiquitous bougainvillea were explosions of bright red, yellow, white and purple bloom smiling in the sun. The numerous old jacarandas carpeted the parched lawn with thousands of purple petals. There were hundreds of shrubs under which I could prowl in a bid to catch birds and scare away any uninvited strange visitors, animal or human, who I suspected would be up to no good. The property was bordered by three white settler neighbours who embraced the reconciliation proffered with the coming of the new dawn.

The hedges dividing two of the properties from ours were punctuated with some gaps which unwelcome intruders into our yard found useful on a few occasions. On the other side was one neighbour with a long asbestos wall stretching all round to their main gate which stood adjacent to ours. The gate we inherited was a rickety, rusty iron contraption that gave no protection to unwelcome intruders, nor to pedestrians in the feeder road from my zealous attention. I did not worry much about tight walls and fool-proof gates for obvious reasons.

At the previous address, I had acquired a cherished habit of making brief visits outside our open yard to meet friends for play, or a growl at them to exert my authority over them. The prospect of losing that indulgence filled me with dread. Otherwise, I really liked the new home so much, that sometimes in those early days I would pause, take a deep breath and think to myself,

"I think I'm going to like it here very much!"

But that didn't mean I did not miss the friends I had left behind in the dog community of our previous home. I even traced my way there once to romp with Rona and Boki. I waited outside their yard convinced that at any minute one of them would wander into view. Well, I could not believe what I saw instead. A couple I had never seen before came out of the house and cantered to splash into the oval swimming pool chasing each other in the pale blue water. They were young, bouncing with energy and full of a zest for life. But all that did not interest me. My thoughts were with Rona and Boki and so I lingered at the gate a moment longer, scanning from afar all the places they used to frequent. Still, there was no sign of my friends.

Disappointed, I made for the shopping centre, thinking of home. The place was as usual throbbing with life and filled with lots of shoppers and loiterers. But there was nothing I found exciting and worth hanging around for. So I decided to proceed to my new home.

One of the landmarks was the veterinary surgery. I kept to the left of this big busy road leading from the town centre through three suburbs to a province out in the country. Somewhere down the line I got confused and lost my bearings. I panicked and started wandering from street to street as if in a dream and losing hope of ever getting back home. I had got to that state of mind when suddenly I heard mum shout, "Shungu, Shungu!" There she was, her head slightly straining through the driver's window. Just as she pulled the car to a stop, Kate, opened the car door for me and I jumped in. "

Shungu, no! We don't live here anymore, you naughty so and so! Come, jump into the car. How did you get here? I feared we would never find you!" Kate sounded really thrilled as she patted my back. I was so happy to see them too and expressed it through my body language as I looked at the moving scenery outside the car window.

I had another passing glimpse of the veterinary surgery but to my eternal relief we whizzed past it from a distance just as I started giving in to my fear of the vet. Within ten minutes the familiar sight of our suburb came into view and soon we entered the new property. Mum ignored me completely as she drove in silence. By now I knew what she was telling me when she adopted that attitude and I did not like it much.

Then, to drive her message home more effectively she had me tethered to the mango tree near our car park for the rest of the day. Sean and the girls came down on mum protesting against such a measure even if it was meant to protect me from being fatally injured in a road accident. The children did not make much of mum's desperate explanations.

"Mum, you see, if a dog is forced into confinement like this, or closed up, it becomes fiercely aggressive and may start to attack and brutalise people, even us your children, not to mention you and dad. Do you want that?" argued Sean, with the girls assenting.

"But that's what I fear he might do to members of the public apart from him getting crushed by traffic. That's my fear, you see. Besides, it is illegal for dogs to wander out unaccompanied by the owner."

"Mum, release Shungu. What has he done? Has he bitten anybody? Please mum," pleaded Sean.

"Yes, mum, that's cruel now," Kate protested her palm wiping tears from her sensitive eyes.

"Very well then, I will release Shungu later. Right now give him his food and water and come up with suggestions of how to stop him from wandering out of the gate," mum asserted. Meanwhile, I had been kicking up a fuss, barking and struggling to free myself to show my utter dislike of any attempt to curtail my freedom of movement in or outside the homestead.

Soon after my meal I sank into such a deep sleep until midnight, when I woke up so refreshed and bursting with energy. Above all, I found with much joy, that I had been let loose from the hated tether. I frisked about in disbelief and resumed my usual trot around the vast yard of our home. Of course, in the morning I went to see the family off to work and school. They were happy to see me free again and I enjoyed some brief moments of sober interaction with Sean, ever generous with the sweet words that had become music to my ears: 'good boy.'

Chapter Six

Settling in the New Neighbourhood

I loved the set up at the house and indeed the whole neighbourhood. However, I found myself unable to take long snoozes after meals as I did before. Being curious, there was so much to keep me active, including insects to paw at as I frisked about on my own in the vastness of the yard.

One sultry afternoon I was stalking a pigeon when I spotted a black cat in our yard, presumably from the property next door. It was perched on a firm branch of a bougainvillea tree with its large green eyes fixed on me; we locked uncertain glances for a split second. Then I made a move and my visitor emitted a sharp yelp as she bolted back to the security of her yard. That was the beginning of a catch-me-if- you-can game with the cat, my feline lady friend, a game that lasted a long time. Her name was Whisky as I later heard her owner call her.

I should have saved my breath and energy by remembering my genetic inability to climb a tree. This mischievous neighbour always took advantage of her ability to scuttle up a tree of any size. Thus, at each encounter I knew it was a game which held little promise of gratification for me. Nevertheless, I did find consolation in the fact that she would always run away from me and that gave me a sense of immense power and pride.

That was the view I held at first before an experience that opened my eyes as to what mischief cats were capable of. Mum sometimes dried fish procured from a man-made lake near Harare. The family loved bream usually prepared fresh for meals, but to break the monotony, she would slush open, salt and dry several pieces in the scorching sun after blotting away excess water with a paper towel. A dome-shaped wire gauze secured with halved bricks over the fish kept the flies away.

The process started on the roof of a six-foot high tool shed and would finish in the warm section of the oven drying without cooking. To cut a long story short, one mid-morning I caught sight of that black cat very busily chomping at the fish up on the shed roof.

Once she had landed on the roof she got to the fish by sliding the bricks aside and up the wire gauze. One strong bark and the cat was momentarily flustered but in a split second swiftly flew into the air like the bionic cat she was, landing noisily on a nearby mango tree branch. I continued barking fiercely, jumping up in futile attempts to catch the miscreant. I saw her now gearing to escape further but I dived and managed to scratch her hind limbs as she bolted over the wall with a sharp yelp to the safety of her home ground. Meanwhile, mum had come round to investigate the cause of the commotion outside.

She was shocked at the chaotic mess that greeted her but sprang into action to dispose of the remainder of the fish somehow. She never allowed me near fish fearing I would choke from the bones. I was sure; I had given the cat a fright that she was unlikely to forget soon. But then cats always do forget, though but not as instantly as chickens do! Mum had just a fleeting glimpse of me in pursuit and the cat taking the final leap to safety.

Whisky was not the only invader I had to contend with. Dogs of all breeds from the neighbourhood and beyond came in to visit - some from curiosity and a need to size me up. Others intended to sort out the fearsome stranger that had recently appeared on their patch but escaped before they could get at him. They crept gingerly through the gaps in the hedge sometimes as single spies and other times in pairs. But I was too strong for them all and always sent them packing except a few who had become my friends.

We would hitch up on our hind legs then noisily embrace with the fore paws licking each other before trotting together in the colourful yard, all my territory! But soon, before they became too comfortable even my friends knew when to clear off, be it night or daytime. Meanwhile, there had been so many close encounters of the confrontational kind with Whisky. Of course, by now I was well able to identify her scent.

Then one day as I went down for my meal thinking of nothing else but my food, I suddenly sensed the now familiar animal whiff and knew it was her. I paused for a moment and started looking around for her. Where was she? I was expecting to be gripped with rage as usual and readied myself to send her scuttling away. But an unexplained feeling of warmth and sublime tenderness washed all over me.

What's happening to me? Maybe it is because I am hungry right now. I shook my head in disbelief. In minutes, I had consumed all my food and I thought I was back to my old self. The scent from the cat had subsided somewhat and with that, so had her strong hold on me. I curled up in my favourite spot to rest under the cool of the old thick leaved old bougainvillea tree as it was such a blazing hot day.

There seemed to be no end to the mysteries or more appropriately, surprises my new dwelling place seemed to be capable of throwing at me. I just hoped there would be no end to this exciting life. But life has a habit of spawning the rough and the smooth, not in any particular order, to be endured by all creatures, human or animal.

Chapter Seven

Mrs Sharp and the Poodle

One ordinary early afternoon, I realised I had been neglecting the other side of our garden or was it that I was summoned by a strange scent, I could not exactly figure it out. Anyway, I headed for the area starting by the veranda just outside the lounge. As I turned the corner I saw an unfamiliar lady greeting mum.

I hid in the shrubs to determine if she was a friend or foe as my advanced training insisted I do. Just as I concluded it was the former, I noticed a white poodle waddling confidently into the yard. I kept my eyes fixed on this small happy bundle of life sniffing here and there as he went along. There was no way I could have guessed he belonged to the lady now pacing behind mum to sit in the cool of the veranda with her.

There had been all kinds of intruders into our patch since we took residence at the address and so, giving way to instinct, my reaction was swift. I pounced on the poor thing and clamped my teeth into her groin, holding her down. Mum and the lady screamed for me to release the shaken victim. Mum had secured a broom handle and before she hit me with it, I felt a powerful force of water from a hose thudding on my face. It was our new experienced gardener VaRoy who came to the rescue. Immediately,

I released the dog now whimpering in pain from a bleeding gashing wound. Forthwith, the owner who had introduced herself to mum as Mrs. Sharp from a few doors down the road, scooped the wailing poodle into her shaking arms and rushed it to the vet for some first aid to reduce blood loss. I knew I had messed up from mum's reaction and the anguished expression on her face.

Crying uncontrollably, she apologised profusely as she tried to catch up with Mrs. Sharp who was already out of the wicket gate heading back to her house. Mum closed the wicket gate shaking her head with embarrassment. In seconds Mrs Sharp was driving, rushing her dog to the vet. Mum cupped her face in both her hands as if pleading to our creator to intervene and help the poodle live.

She sauntered to the veranda and sat there in stunned silence for a while. Apparently, unlike a good number of white nationals, Mrs Sharp and her family had decided to stay put in new Zimbabwe. She had kindly taken the initiative to come and welcome us to the neighbourhood, and to think I did this shameful thing!

When mum returned to face me I assumed a submissive posture, whimpering as well, to demonstrate my sense of utter shame and regret. Mum ignored me for a while showing her disapproval at my act of aggression, so embarrassing for mum and hurtful for the little dog.

Damn the territorial animal instinct! I couldn't help myself. In spite of all the training to interact better with other dogs, some instinctual urges defied control and the most difficult, I found, was the protection of my own space. After all, I was basically still a dog. I had just settled into a new home after endless trials and tribulations with human and animal intruders, a few with dark intentions. Now I had to start all over again; I was bound to be anxious and stressed, at least for a while.

The poodle was not detained at the vet and mum was relieved to see her some days later waddling about happily in her family yard with the bandage still on. It was only because the wicket gate had been mistakenly left open.

Mrs Sharp had taken the opportunity to enter our premises to make the noble and welcoming gesture to the new neighbours. Years later, the youngest girls from the two families met at the same secondary school. Thembi and Sue would talk about the incident with Sue assuring Thembi that her mum took some

responsibility for bringing in the poodle without prior warning when she knew of the existence of Shungu.

Sue explained further that as soon as the little dog was well on the road to recovery, her mum put the incident behind her and was happy again. During one school holiday, I saw Thembi leading Mrs Sharp's daughter Sue into our yard amidst girly giggles and that was alright with me.

Once I realised human visitors were welcome or saw them fraternising together with any of my family, I was somewhat welcoming too but remained vigilant at a distance. However, with animals including dogs, it was another matter. The reaction was instantaneous.

It was more for this reason than my compulsive tendency to wander that the vet advised I be castrated. After some reluctance mum and dad took me for the operation. Medical intervention proved more effective at reducing aggression than in tempering my propensity to wander out of our yard unaccompanied. Call it what you may but wander lust it was certainly not.

Why? Because I did not just take off daily like some mad dog. But after a few weeks trotting around in the yard much of the time and snoozing here and there I needed a change of environment.

And so I made a decision, as rationally as it was possible to as a dog, to go meet my dog friends out there. I loved the walks with family on the lead, but it just was not the same. Everything was too formal and rather restricted. The inclination, which started during my earlier life at the unwalled rented house, had hardened into some kind of a habit. I found myself trotting outside in the neighbourhood, following on the path I had already marked as my territory either on my way to visit one or two dog friends or on accompanied walks on the lead.

Through that earlier freedom, in time, I had learnt to control the urge to harass dogs and people I passed on the way. The poodle remains the only creature, human or animal I ever badly gored whether inside our yard or out on my stolen walks. Otherwise, I would have been put down a long time ago like one of my nemeses in the neighbourhood of our old address.

The bulldog had badly gored two cycling domestic workers within a period of six months. Lucky enough, she had been vaccinated against several infections including rabies. The first victim was treated in casualty at a local hospital but limped in bandages for some weeks before he could resume work.

The second and older victim had to be admitted at the same hospital due to the seriousness of his wounds. The dog owner was held to account and made to pay compensation and fines in accordance with the law of the land The other effect my castration had was that my interest in female dogs was reduced, but the urge still throbbed in me from time to time, though to a lesser degree. But what had been removed with absolute finality by castration was my ability to father puppies.

As far as I can recall my training started some weeks after I joined my human family at our previous address. Back then Sean had started with the use of simple library training manuals. But after the incident with the poodle mum ordered that training be veered up a gear and be more regular and consistent.

It was no longer limited to following such simple commands like "fetch," "sit," "stay," and others with immediate reward for me. From now on it was decided to go as far professional as possible. This meant resorting to the services of special dog trainers. The practice was for the dog owners to watch a demonstration of training in whatever area the dog was intended to serve.

I was brought into the family to be a watchdog. There would be some practical sessions; as many as a family could afford to pay for. The major on-going dog training practice would be carried out at home both formally and through life experiences. Sticking to regular training proved much more of a challenge than mum and dad had anticipated. This was in the early 80s with children still in primary and secondary schools.

Mum and dad were still juggling their demanding occupations with school runs. But during those windows of opportunity which availed themselves, my training became more serious and regular than in the past. Again, Sean embraced the responsibility for my training program. I liked this young man who became my best friend from the day I started my life with this family.

We played lots of games together and even when Mum took me to The Botanic Gardens on a lead with the three children on most weekends, Sean walked me monitoring my behaviour. He re-enforced desired actions and re-actions immediately with my favourite treats, patting me as he praised me for good behaviour. For any positive reaction, I executed on encounter with other dogs hostile and friendly ones, Sean or dad would immediately stroke, embrace, affectionately rumple or give me food treats such as dog biscuits and others to reinforce the behaviour.

Food treats were alright but that meant a bit less food at lunch as a form of dietary control. But on the rare occasion that Sean or mum considered it was safe to, they stretched a point and allowed my usual amount of food.

"Ok, ok but don't make a habit of it. Have that then," she would caution pointing a finger as she tossed an extra treat indulgently. If she was in an expansive mood she would add a pat and a rub of my neck into the bargain. Mum had resumed being my friend, not very long after I embarrassed her by attacking the poodle. She had ignored me soon afterwards to avoid giving me the wrong message by reinforcing my horrible and aggressive behaviour. I had longed to hear her calling Shungu.

Then with a smile and rumple she asked me, "Where have you been? We all wanted to see you." Sometimes I would run out of the yard for one reason or another or just for the fun of it. On several occasions mum came out walking or driving to look for me and found me just running along alone or with a dog friend. As soon as I heard her cheery voice I would gallop to her and we would get home together with me secure and basking in her presence.

Of course, being a dog, I would now and again sniff about, take short diversions to attend to creepy crawlies including flying gnats and other such insects or water one or two lamp posts and bushes bordering the road.

Every member of this family treated me with warmth and reassurance which made me happy. I was a consummate sucker for praise and a tender touch. I should make it clear, though my family did not approve of my stolen excursions out there, they must have realised how lonely I was and that each time a family member came out to look for me, I would be spotted doing no mischief or harm but mingling with other clean well looked after dogs whose parents could not yet afford to tightly fence them in their property. It was a source of much relief to me that my family were not firm believers in keeping me tethered to a tree all day or locked up in a shed.

How would I route unwelcome intruders on our property whilst I was restrained? I always remembered how terrible I felt that day when I shocked the driver of the removal van with my fierce barking. The family had no alternative but to have me tied to the guava tree. It was horrendous to say the least. I had always tried hard to avoid a repeat of such restraint.

But if I allowed myself to be a veritable nuisance and go about biting humans and other animals willy-nilly, I was bound to be restrained one way or another.

Chapter Eight

Not Always Like Cats and Dogs!

It was not possible to tell how many family members were aware of my new found cat friend. When I think about it though, mum had a glimpse of Whisky escaping into her home grounds after our previous encounter which could hardly be viewed as a friendly one. She might have cringed at the thought of me tearing the cat apart, upsetting her cordial relations with yet another neighbour. She could never have guessed the changes in my feelings for Whisky. I now hoped no one knew because at that moment Whisky seemed to have slipped away from me for good. That was what I had hoped for soon after the fish incident. But feelings do change and mine were no exception. This mounting curiosity or interest in Whisky became one of my sweet little secret agonies that kept my dog mind active and alive.

I had not had sight of Whisky for quite a long while now and somehow could not stop myself from looking up the trees to see if she was either perched up on any branch that stretched out from their yard into ours, or on the wall demarcating the properties. I couldn't understand what was happening to me. I liked thinking of her and missed her beautiful green eyes, with their charm and touching vulnerability.

I had heard a solemn song which mum used to hum along too absent-mindedly, usually whilst we were out driving. The words of the chorus were, 'When will I see you again?' This was some time ago at the old house when I was rather as dead to tender emotions as a stegosaurus. I take that back because that wasn't quite true. Dinosaurs, as I learnt later in my life, had an amazing capacity for group living and the parents nursed their young for much longer than many other animal species, probably including dogs. So they must have a tender and caring disposition.

The tune and what it was all about found its way into my memory and repeated itself uninvited filling me with an overwhelming wish to see Whisky. I was tormented, each time I heard the two dogs next door chasing her. I shook with helpless anger but there was nothing I could do to help her. I would then console myself by remembering how quick she scuttled up trees. From up a lofty distance, she hissed scornfully at them as they shuttled down below her on the ground.

She would always beat them to it and tease them from the safety of a higher perch. Bullies! But then I wondered why she no longer revealed herself to me. Oh, how I needed to see her! And again, that haunting piece of music! Whisky, where are you?

Then, starting as if from afar rising up to a crescendo, "Miao, miao, mew!" Whisky continued to cry or call, I could not make out which. But try as hard as I could to trace where the sound came from, whether from up a tree branch in our yard or another over on Whisky's side of the wall, she remained invisible. So near and yet so far way! Disappointed, I sauntered to have some rest, steeped in self-pity for having no friends nearer home.

Of course, I stopped myself descending so abysmally low in loneliness as to start intoning, 'All….by… my…self' There would have been no need for getting that far because I had a few friends up the road. It was only at that moment that there was a need in me to socialise with my close neighbour Whisky. I needed an animal friend nearer home.

I just wanted her to know I was not the bully I feared she might have taken me to be after I routed her from the fish she was enjoying that day. The goings on in the next yard continued. It went on for over two weeks during which time I managed to settle back into my usual daily routine of loneliness.

One morning, I was feeling down and rather physically drained when mum called me. After she inspected me for fleas, ticks and

checked my general wellbeing, I lay down for a short rest. The rest turned out to be longer than intended. Imagine my utter joy when I opened my eyes and there she was looking so serene though a bit apprehensive. The large green eyes reflected so much tenderness, my heart missed a beat. I realised that was why my sleep was dreamless, so deep and so peaceful. She was right there with me! Her fur soothing me! At that point I knew we would share some blessed time together.

Just as I figured out how to break the ice with her she playfully pawed at my side ever so gently, challenging me to a game of cats and dogs. We fell into step and indulged in all sorts of antics-hide and seek and chasing each other. It was joyous and beautiful. A lasting brother-sister truce was sealed then. After that Whisky jumped the wall bordering her yard and mine whenever she felt the need for more interaction or frisking about with a friendly neighbour.

There were a few times we just lay in the mutual warmth of muted friendship, secure and uplifted. But being a dog I could not scale the wall into her yard, at least, that was what I thought. That was why I never met the dogs of our immediate neighbour to the west of our property. However, we often communicated what feelings we had for each other in the way that animals did. It was always my fervent hope that they did not hurt my dear friend.

Since Whisky and I also fought from time to time there seemed no reason to dislike them. It was gratifying to know that with Whisky, after a scuffle, the reconciliation was sweet, especially after the long cooling off period when we would miss each other. But, of course, we did not deliberately get into scuffles to achieve that end.

It was wonderful to know there was such a friend nearby because what we shared, though platonic, was sublime. It was good to know I was no longer alone, this side of the neighbourhood.

Chapter Nine

The Wall Rises

Several years passed since we moved to the present house and a lot had happened in my dog life. It was clear to me as I matured in age that nature endowed me with a small strong stature characteristic of the Staffordshire bull terrier breed. Mine is an ordinary dog face with brown-black intelligent eyes softening a hard-set core head and strong, powerful jaws. I was proud of my glistening black fur with a white patch that ran from under my neck down to my chest. My legs were firm, robust and strong through much exercise. Ever since I was young I had to chase marauding dogs and unwelcome humans as part of my guard duties, in addition to trotting about on the property sometimes for no particular reason.

On moving house mum and dad had a plan to have a strong wall constructed around the property. But this was delayed by some technicality pertaining to the boundary between one of the two properties on the eastern side of the house.

In time this was resolved amicably by the local authority of the area. Without any further delay, dad commissioned a reputable company of emerging businessmen in Harare to build the asbestos panel wall. The wall was to rise on the three boundaries, which at that time were not properly fortified, but bounded by hedges with gaps in places. In no time the work had started and a six-foot high wall could be seen rapidly rising from the main gate, stretching and turning to separate the properties on the eastern side of our yard.

I had some misgivings about this high wall which was sure to fence me in and effectively interfere with my short strolls outside our yard. In other words, I had two minds about the whole thing. I had got used to a freedom most dogs in the area did not enjoy. Their parents did not take them for long enough walks, or regular ones for that matter.

With my family, dog walking never stuck to a rigid schedule. Presumably, because there was so much space in our yard to trot and frisk about, they thought I had enough exercise. I loved going out for walks with the family but I simply hated the leads no matter how beautiful or comfortable they were. Sometimes I would, without making it obvious, squint up my eyes to read mum's or dad's face.

Quite a few times I had the impression they felt as restricted as I was. Despite this, I still struggled between a craving for a free trot and a wish to be in my parents' company. Sean was different. He often took me to a long and quiet road leading to a trodden grass patch. He would unclip the lead from the collar. Rumpling me he would say, "Shungu now, let's go." We would run to the end of the road, where we then strayed further into the grass-covered patch till we were both breathless with exhaustion. On our way back home, Sean would only clip back the lead when pedestrians appeared.

I simply loved those times with Sean and wished we could stay out longer. My watchdog experience had shown me that high walls were not much of a deterrent when it came to skilled, hardened crooks, but those walls would certainly increase the chances of the crooks being caught, whilst trying to escape with booty. So it could be conceded that walls constructed around homesteads had limited usefulness beyond aesthetics and defining the boundary between   properties.

It seemed as if any protective measures meant nothing to thieves' intent on stealing. These were the same people who did not think twice to poison a dog they considered ferocious and watch it writhe and twist in pain before bashing it to death and proceeding on to their dark business.

At one time, there was a craze which involved drugging the

property owners and their families while they slept in their bedrooms at night. The hardened desperados then waited till they were dead sure the drug had taken effect before they sprung into a 'Mission Impossible' dare devil action. They would then break in, heave or even roll the unconscious family members from their beds on to the carpets and go on to strip them of their nighties and pyjamas for good measure.

One house-proud family had property bought on hire purchase and when everything had been delivered, the family could not contain their pride showing off their new possession to friends and relations. But soon a visit by the said notorious crooks delivered the family a shattering blow. They woke up in an embarrassing state of undress to a house nearly emptied of the new furniture, including a colour television and special kitchen gadgetry!

I had a most trying time when the wall was being put up. There was a lot of building and renovating and other construction work going on in most parts of the country. This required building equipment and materials. In time, ordinary residents unable to afford the astronomical prices resorted to desperate measures including theft to procure building material. It was indeed, a difficult time in my life but I faced up to the challenge. The builders must have regarded affluent suburbs as being immune to crime.

Unfortunately, this assumption commonly held by many people rendered the builders careless with the building materials. Instead of putting away the unused material from the worksite at the end of each day, they left it exposed. What they should have been doing was storing the unused material in the main storage shed as they had been advised.

Ordinarily, I was always suspicious of anyone who wasn't a family member physically picking things up from the ground, or female friends of gardeners taking dry laundry from the line outside. I cannot remember how many times the new gardener's wife had to run back into their cabin and shut me out. Sometimes a family member had to be around anyone picking anything in the yard that is if they had any idea where I was hiding.

When work on the wall started, dad had to be around to make

sure that I saw him talking and laughing with the builders who would assemble the equipment and material they planned to use during the day before dad left for work.

I would be assured for the most part of the day that dad approved of them shifting things around. I would hang around for a little while longer though after everyone had left. Eventually, when I got used to workers engaged in tasks in our yard, I stopped being suspicious of them and soon enough, they could safely pick up anything anywhere in the yard for use, once it was used within the yard. If I spotted any of them alone at any time stealthily lifting anything, I would presume they were up to no good.

Without much ado, I would silently prowl forward and inflict a nip on the arm or leg. Invariably, the stolen object was instantly dropped in panic as the thief fled. Once or twice I had nipped a stranger who had come into our yard without invitation and attempted to pick something up, even if it was their own equipment or tool box. I remember one afternoon a mechanic, Mr Nzira, arrived around lunch-time.

He had been expected to come in much earlier, around 11:00am. Mum had taken a few days off from work. As the cook and gardener had taken their lunchbreak, there was only mum to show the mechanic where the borehole that needed repairs was situated. I had actually seen mum showing the mechanic where the engine was situated. My curiosity was piqued and I hid in the dark of some shrubs a distance from the borehole shed. Neither of them saw me. I could see everything the mechanic was doing clearly and kept my eyes fixed on him.

"Our dog has a thing about strangers in our yard picking up anything, especially a bag or box of tools. I mean that black dog you have just seen. I don't know where he has disappeared to though. If I call it now him, he will come straight for you. So when you finish repairing the borehole just call me. Now, if you could pull the tool box near the engine, or is it a motor?" Mum asked.

"Motor, yes," Mr Nzira replied. "I'm in the kitchen and I'll open the window wider so that I hear you call. Leave your tool box on the ground. He won't touch you if you do that because he has seen you with me but he is watching right now. Ok then."

"Yes, Mrs Mabvira I understand very well."

When Mr Nzira finished repairing the borehole, he replaced his tools in the tool box, locked it and stood up. He remembered not to pick up the toolbox. But what does he proceed to do? He could see mum through the open window but did not call her. He looked around for me. Then he decided that since he could not see me I must have been at the other side of the massive building.

No, he was not going to bother amai, he decided. Mum was by the kitchen sink peeling potatoes. Mr Nzira's eyes went down to the tool box. He checked for me one last time and I thought, "No, he is not going to do anything stupid, surely," I said to myself in disbelief. I could not believe what I saw next! Mr. Nzira stooped to pick the tool box and instantly I nipped his hand near the elbow and then just walked away. He then called out to mum, examining the scratch on his hand.

"But Mr Nzira…I warned you about the black dog! Let's see," mum examined the wound.

"Mrs Mabvira, really you shouldn't worry. You warned me and the wound is just a little deeper than a scratch," Mr Nzira said,

"Yes, it's a very shallow wound. But I apologise for this. He is usually a good dog but sometimes he gets confused. He was vaccinated for rabies which is a good thing, but it does not make it right," Mum reassured him.

"I'll clean the wound with boiled water and a little Dettol." "Oh no, Mrs Mabvira, please excuse me. There's no time for all that. I have an appointment with the next customer and I daren't be late again. My job exposes me to this sort of risk. This is not the first time it has happened to me," he explained picking up the tool box to leave. Mum came up in goose pimples as she feared for him.

She feared a recurrence of the incident. I noticed her heave a sigh of relief when I did not re-emerge from wherever I was, and, like a snake lurking in the grass, inflict another bite, probably a nasty one this time.

"I'll take you to the gate. How far are you going now?" Mum offered.

"Greystone Park. I'll be there in just over forty minutes, taking short cuts on my bike," said Mr. Nzira as he wheeled his bike out through the open wicket gate after securing his toolbox at its rear end. I had hidden myself again where I could see and hear mum's voice, but this time with some remorse as well as confusion.

On her way back from the gate she noticed I had joined the other dogs. She called the other dogs but not my name. I realised she was not happy with me at all. I knew that what I had done would take away the smile from her face for a while. But what was I supposed to do? I wished situations did not happen. I was inclined to forget that some things belonged to other people and not always to my human family. I would not have the capacity to remember the tool box was brought by the mechanic.

As a loyal dog I was duty bound to ensure that my family's belongings were safe. The problem was that I wasn't always able to make the distinction. But I knew picking up was central to stealing. This sometimes put me in difficult situations such as the most recent one.

Well, some days were going to be good and others not so great! Life was full of ups and downs. I decided to curl up to sleep; tomorrow was another day. There was a strong wild tree with branches spreading out at a safe height away from the reach of dogs outside our gate.

This tree had become a refuge for quite a few unwelcome human intruders - a refuge from me and other dogs in the immediate neighbourhood. At times, even innocent passers-bye had found themselves clambering up the tree for refuge on hearing any furious dog bark even when no dog in the neighbourhood was in actual pursuit.

To their credit, none of the workers on our wall were foolish enough to be tempted to steal and risk my fury. Pilfering by workers was a frequent occurrence at building sites though often the acts remained undiscovered. One hot night, a nocturnal visitor who had escaped me ended up in the wild tree of refuge. He had let himself through the unlocked gate and walked down the driveway to the bags of cement held in a temporary, make-shift storage space.

He had left the driveway, picked up a bag of cement and was now running stealthily up to the gate with it perched on his left shoulder when I spotted him. This time I barked as I went after him. He was a fast runner. His strides were long and in no time he was struggling to balance his slipping feet between two branches of the tree. I continued to try and reach him as I jumped higher each time. I was sure he was shaking with nerves. I could hear his shallow quickened breathing. I was not going to give up on him. I ran, tossed up and down around the tree barking like mad and threatening to bite.

All the while, I looked up, my eyes fixed on the dark struggling form looming between leaves. Soon I detected a form approaching the gate from inside our yard.

"What's the matter, Shungu? Who opened the gate?" Dad asked as he peered with the torchlight into the thick leafed tree. I maintained a furious bark.

"Hey! Who's that? Come down!" dad ordered on catching sight of the thief. "The dog will not bite while I am here.

Get down! What were you doing? This dog will not behave like this if you were completely innocent. Shungu be quiet! Stay!" dad ordered. I managed to hold my breath and cool down to obey dad's third "stay" command. I was still shaking with anger. With much trepidation, the stranger jumped down the tree.

I shall never know what lies the crook told dad once on the ground. The whole episode ended in no time. None of the neighbours had been drawn out to the streets to enquire about the dogs bark-talking so much. My dog supporters kept on barking long after I had calmed down but not with as much fury as I had vented.

While dad closed the manual gate, I took the lead towards

home and waited for him by the bag of cement which had been dumped under one of the palm trees mum planted some years ago, and which were growing fast skywards vying for oxygen and sunshine.

Dad was incensed on realising he had been hood-winked into releasing the thief. That bag now under the palm tree told dad the whole story which my dog genetics would not have allowed me to tell. He was, however, certain the thief would not dare return tonight or any other night for some time to come, if ever. He lingered temporarily in thought by the bag of cement the thief had cast by the palm tree.

After shaking his head several times, he heaved the bag, took a few strides and dropped it on top of the pile of other cement bags. All the bags would be moved to an unused garage in the morning. The night was cool and dry. So I curled myself by the pile of cement bags to rest and soon I was asleep. In the morning there was much talk about the events of the previous night. I was always filled with awe and expectation each time I was led inside the house.

"Shungu, come," mum beckoned re-enforcing with a hand. A communication sign I had become familiar with.

She was standing at the open kitchen door and her body language was telling me that she was very pleased with me somehow. A typical case of saying more when nothing had been said at all.

Of course, I would soon know what that was all about. I jumped and trotted up to her with a feeling of exhilaration. Her face was all smiles as she led me through the spacious kitchen, past a vast dining-room into the double lounge. Mum took her position besides dad.

"Shungu, sit. Good boy," started dad.

The children, who had been getting ready for school, all rushed into the lounge shouting

"Shungu, Ah!! Shungu, good boy." Sean came and knelt before me as usual patting my cheeks.

Mum's brother came in shaking his head in disbelief with a wide smile. Dad had shared the event of the previous night with the family at breakfast before retiring in the lounge for the early news.

After the main part of the news, the TV was kept on at muted volume. Years ago, when I was still young, I would have stationed myself in front of the TV, close to the screen, barking my throat sore at the unseeing newsreader or whatever was on. It was worse if a dog was featured.

"This dog is so good; I have never met one like Shungu before. He behaves like a person, so reliable," said mum's brother, as he lavished praises on me in mum and dad's presence.

I had grown to like that guy. He handled me with some respect just like my family. But sometimes I suspected fear had a part to play in the way he was so ingratiating towards me, though I was still flattered. Well, tell me a dog that does not suck up to praise, let alone pile upon pile of it!

Dad stood up and patting me lightly said, "Come, your biscuits. Children, go to the car. I'm coming."

"Umm scrumptious, that was nice," I thought licking my lips. I went round to see dad and the children off to school and work respectively.

On his way out he invited the supervisor of the builders to come near him and emphatically reminded him to ensure all the building material was safely out of reach of marauding thieves. I curled myself in my usual cool place under the shade of a palm tree. Intermittently, I kept a vigilant watch over the wall. Builders now regarded me with some fear flavoured with respect.

They had come to know that they could not mess about with me in the yard. However, I kept playing back in my mind the scene in the lounge this morning. I loved it when I made mum and dad smile with happiness. I bet as those memories went viral in my head my face wore a big warm dog smile.

I had learned which behaviour of mine pleased mum and dad and my memory helped me to remember to look for the opportunities to please them, so I could be rewarded in the way I was used to, the way that made me feel good. This was how mum and dad and the family children came to think of me that, as an individual dog, I had a 'personality' resembling that of humans in some way. I didn't exactly think like them but there was a dog way of interpreting human body and sign language which enriched the interaction between us.

They conveyed this by their expressions and in their interactions with me. I hated it when I displeased my parents which resulted in them ignoring me. So I kept in line whenever I could. You see, contrary to the view commonly held by many humans, dogs are not entirely brainless.

We have an ability to size up situations and come up with strategies to meet challenges, achieve goals, even higher abstract ones, some more than others. Many dogs in the world have earned their owners' respect in their own different ways, some to a greater degree than others even within the same breed. I am not at all unique in that regard.

Chapter Ten

Shumba and Sheba Join the Family Pack

The six-foot high wall around the property was completed within three to four months. It took that long because of shortages of supplies and delays in deliveries. Actually there were only three long sides to be walled because the long border with the property from which Whisky emerged, boasted a robust, fool-proof wall topped with barbed wire. The white settler family on that property included a pleasant widow who had long retired from farming and received frequent visits from her adult children and their families. They had endured several break-ins including a terrifying armed robbery during which their safe was emptied of the treasured family possessions as well as some cash.

I was now walled-in but that did not stop me entirely from traversing further than my prescribed geographical area. The new six-foot gate consisted of close iron rods spiked at the top. It was held together lengthwise by equally strong rods expertly installed so that I could not escape through either side of the gate like before.

The wicket gate beside this main gate was kept locked at all times. The workers had been supplied with the keys so that they were assured of free movement in and out of the homestead. But the main gate was operated manually like the majority of homestead gates during the mid-eighties. Mum or dad would have to come out of the car when going out and open the gate.

Most of the time I would listen and stay inside but on rare occasions I felt a strong urge to shoot out and run ignoring the

calls to get back. I would not get very far before I complied and trotted back into the yard allowing the gate to be closed. I must admit I was wrecked with anxiety whenever mum and dad drove out and spent some time hanging around the gate area awaiting their return.

But as time went by I felt more secure in the knowledge that they would return sooner or later because they usually came back home to the children and I. There was a lady friend of mine, Tessa, six gates down the road who had just had puppies which I could not have fathered because of my neutered state.

She was one of a few female friends I 'dillydallied' with since we moved to the present property - a good neighbour and friend. I had been spending some time with the six puppies after the owners of the house left for work. They always chased me away when they were around but their domestic workers left us alone. Then I noticed the puppies seemed to be getting less and less in number.

When I showed up again a few days later, the last two puppies were nowhere to be seen. Tessa seemed to have sunk into a depression. She was sad and all forlorn. I had a good glimpse of Tessa lying just outside her kennel, her eyes closed.

I waited willing her to wake up and acknowledge my presence. I was also hoping to see the little ones waddling back to dive at her breasts, a spectacular sight I had started looking forward to on my brief visits. Just as I started turning to leave I saw Tessa's eyes open, her head raised looking unseeingly in the air. It seemed by now she had lost all hope of seeing the puppies again. I could tell she was aware of my presence but she was still shattered by her loss. Infact, bereft, she was not interested in my visit either. I lingered there for a few more minutes, but still no puppies came to their mother.

Then it dawned on me that they had gone for good! Sold! All of them! I was overwhelmed with sadness and with a heavy heart, I trudged back home. I knew though that soon I would see Tessa again. It was common practice for suburban dog-owners to raise some cash by advertising six to eight-month-old puppies in the local papers for sale. I am convinced that is how I came to be in mum's car that day when she dropped me to my first steps on the soil of our yard at the old rented house. I made straight for my kennel thinking of those beautiful and tender darlings with their glistening black and tan fur with sparse white patches. I was miserable and weak with shock so much so that Whisky had to leave when she found me not much of a companion, nor responsive to chasing games. In my mind, I was for a moment transported back in time to the afternoon Tessa and I chased the car thief together up to a main road that ran through the suburb into the hinterland. Mum had taken me for a long walk on a lead to our local shops.

On the way there I remember passing a man who looked unkempt leaning on the tree outside Tessa's home just opposite the ungated entrance into the yard. Mr Brown, the car owner had dashed into his home and to pick some papers he needed that afternoon, as he had forgotten to take them with him in the morning, rushing to work. He parked the car at the entrance of his yard and noticed this man who avoided eye contact. Mr Brown had deliberately left the car stalling because he was just going to pick the papers and drive back to his office.

Mum and I had just turned the corner from the shops and spotted someone black reversing the familiar car. Mr Brown was flustered. He knew straight away at the first glance that this was car theft as there had been many reports of such everywhere in Harare at that time. He tried to stop the driver flapping the papers around. I jacked loose from mum and barking, joined Tessa in pursuit of the car. As the car approached and crossed Mazoe Road we knew, except for a miracle, we could not catch it and so, as if by telepathy, we automatically turned at the same time and ran back together panting, crest fallen. We crouched where mum and Mr Brown stood flabbergasted by the theft.

Mum kept repeating, "I saw the young guy leaning nonchalantly on that tree."

"Yes, I saw him too as I got out of the car but it never occurred to me that he was a crook," said Mr Brown as he now strode past mum and crossed the road to enter his un-gated yard towards his house.

His wife came forward to thank me and mum for stopping by to help. "I have already contacted the police," said Mrs Brown. "I hope the car will be found," Mum empathised as we walked home.

Tessa had followed Mr Brown into their yard. That was long before Tessa had puppies. Some time had passed after Tessa's puppies were sold. But thank goodness she soon got over the gradual disappearance of her little ones. Whenever opportunity presented itself we met in the feeder road from my home and tenderly nuzzled as we had always done. I was sure, several months after her sad loss, she had now been spayed. She no longer emitted that scent which had drawn male dogs to her.

On the other hand, chances to meet her became achingly less as a wire net enclosure had been erected at the back of the house to hold me in when cars left home in the mornings. The wicket wire gate would then be opened to free me for the day. I would be sitting impatiently with my tongue out and my tail wagging faster than the ticking of a clock. As soon as the little gate opened I shot out barking and then get lost in surveillance around the home yard.

This arrangement was soon abandoned through fear of rendering me more aggressive than I already was. The gardener had reported to my parents that he feared my increasing temper each time he braved himself to open the improvised wire gate. Sometimes I was lucky when Whisky made an appearance and we would play around enjoying a few games. At times if I had other priorities on my mind and Whisky was in a playing mood,

I quickly got rid of her. A throaty growl would send her up some leafy trees to peer back at me from a safe height, her wide green eyes hot with rebuke. If the object of my attention was outside I would turn my eyes onto the bolted gate in front of me trying to figure out how I was ever going to climb over the most annoying barrier ever.

I trotted to and from along the length of the main gate and part of the wall. All the while I was also jumping desperately as I barked in response to Tessa's barking call outside. I could not believe it when I realised there was no way out now that the 'barricade' stood firmly all around the property. After a while, the barking outside ceased, the beckoning had stopped. I knew then she must have gone elsewhere. I then wondered if the barking had indeed been Tessa.

Feeling defeated I found my way to my backyard. I totally forgot all about Whisky. Whether she was still observing me from a perch up nearby or had retreated deep into her yard, I did not care much right then. She served herself well to get the message and keep away from me. I just wanted to curl up in one of my favourite spots and rest before the gardener called me for my meal. Not that I kept track of clock time, but a combination of factors pointed that way.

Around midday my tummy often rumbled triggering in me a craving for food. VaRoy himself was very good with meal times. He resented preparing the bowl while I waited, watching him with threatening impatience. I had been feeling so lonely for some time as I was now imprisoned. I found myself inside the great wall surrounding. Whisky must have become unsure of my moods. She was disinclined to risk another rebuff and rejection by me. In fact, I had nothing but respect and admiration for her persistent loyalty for even before that fateful day she had experienced a taste of my unfair treatment of her on a number of occasions. But she would still pay me a visit after a period of absence, during which I sometimes had to endure disturbing loneliness. Then one Saturday morning mum drove in with Sean and his sisters. She was using the truck that day. As the truck came to a stop in the garage I thought I caught dog-type scent and then my ears prickled.

"Can that be true? Squeaking and squealing puppies?" I wondered.

I was already barking nervously when Sean emerged from the back of the van and as he dropped down from the van, he firmly ordered me to sit still. He made straight for me and patting me, clipped the lead on and quickly walked me to the enclosure as I continued to protest.

Meanwhile, mum carried a dog basket containing the two squealing puppies to the scullery where she served them bowls of fresh commercial meats she had left thawing to room temperature. I was consciously aware that my family feared that, driven by jealousy, I might run amok and cause significant harm to the puppies. I had to curb the compelling power of the animal territorial instincts and not cause any chaos. I had done well so far except, of course, the uncalled for incident involving the poodle. Sean named the male puppy Shumba and the female one Sheba. They were both 7 weeks old Alsatians, healthy looking and beautiful.

Sean had trained me to avoid unnecessary confrontations, except in pursuit of my watch-dog duties. Of course, the family had to be careful not to give the puppies much more attention, in my presence in case I got jealous and harmed the puppies. I was given my food soon after my family had-had their meal and before the puppies had theirs and that gave me a lovely feeling of power and dominance over the little ones. That ranking order suited my fancies of self-worth perfectly.

Dad still brought bones for me, sometimes fresh with bits of meat on them and other times dry ones to strengthen my teeth. Otherwise they got their teeth into any objects they came-across; shoes, plastic utensils and sofas. As usual I got my bones first and went crazy gnawing and crushing them with my strong teeth.

After, assessing my behaviour in the puppies' presence for a number of weeks, mum was satisfied that I did not pose much risk to them. The release of the puppies outside was done carefully in stages and soon we started playing together. Sean had been exposing them to me gradually under his watchful eye as we snuggled together in growing mutual trust.

I began to feel really great around these puppies as they aroused the paternal instinct in me which was frustrated when Tessa's puppies were sold one after the other, after I had fought hard over eight weeks to gain Tessa's trust. Just as she started allowing me to get closer to them all, they had gone. I was soon guiding and teaching Sheba and

Shumba to cope with their environment. I was virtually a father to them, growling at and nudging them when they misbehaved or rewarding them when they were well behaved. They loved playing hide and seek in the nearest shrubs just outside the kitchen, and as they grew older their play area widened.

I let them climb all over me when I rested and we licked each other to soothe an itch or just to clean the puppies. We had become a close family pack. Shumba began to challenge my authority from time to time but a rough nudge or a light bite inflicted anywhere on his tiny body warned him to stop and remember his station. Any repetition of insolence invited a deeper though not significant bite and that did it. Sheba was cautious but learnt faster. She was not cowardly nor would it be accurate to describe her as docile.

I soon formed the impression that she had lots of common sense which inspired her coping skills. So like humans, I learnt over the years, animals did look after each other in times of need and suckled other dogs' puppies, raising and protecting them into adulthood. We are also our brother's keeper, animal style. A little over a year after their arrival, it did not seem appropriate to refer to Shumba and Sheba as puppies. The two dogs had shot up and surpassed me in both height and fullness of stature.

They were both endowed with very healthy appetites. Scuffles over bones decreased with time especially between Shumba and I. But sometimes I could not help the desire to have a go at Shumba's bone just to remind him I was the boss. Mum was determined to play an active role in controlling the portions given to the dogs at their meal time. Sheba and Shumba would gulp down their food so fast that though served first, I would empty my bowl long after they had emptied theirs. Shumba almost dived into his bowl and crunched up his food in no time at all. He would then try to eat my food.

On one occasion he ignored my warning growl and a heated scuffle resulted from which he emerged with a slightly grazed ear. From then on, he became more deferential and quite willing to observe protocol - though not all of the time! The issue of feeding the Alsatians took some time to be resolved.

One big snag was their tendency to lie about with limited inclination to run around unless they decided to follow my lead racing in the yard or on occasion shoot through the main gate

for a run along the road outside and back. It would not be true to give the impression that the other dogs did not act on their own initiative. I admit I had a tendency to blow my own trumpet and think Shumba and Sheba could never be as good as I was at everything. Indeed, they were much more inclined to rest or sleep for prolonged periods, the latter more than the former. But sometimes they did run about chasing each other around the yard without my lead.

The danger of little exercise was weight gain which would become a sure health risk. But mum was determined to keep their diet under control. I never had weight problems mainly because I was energetic, spending most of my time up and about checking on movements, sight or sounds that aroused my curiosity. I also have performed outstanding feats as an overall watch and guard dog on my own but sometimes I benefited from the support of Shumba and Sheba. Unwelcome visitors would set off a groundswell of barking from all of us in our yard, in the neighbourhood dog community and even beyond.

By this time in my life, it had been definitely impressed on my mind that evil indeed flourished at night time. Most of the burglaries and thefts I had foiled occurred then. That was why ever since I became a member of my family, I learnt this quickly and so, up to this day, I found it difficult to sleep easy at night though I did not bark unnecessarily. Even after the protective walls were set up around the homestead I continued night watching intermittently through wakeful sleep. I barked when

I inspected the yard especially if I caught some unusual human scent wafting from outside our great wall. I was committed to that kind of life and had no wish for any other. I was sure my alertness drove many would-be intruders to change their minds and give up the intention to break into our house and rob or hurt the family.

Usually when night fell, the cool refreshing breeze energised and galvanised the whole dog pack of our family into activity. There would be much persuasion for each other to join in the natural dog antics frisking about all over the place and chasing each other barking here and there. Shumba's bark surpassed everyone else's in depth and when he growled he almost sounded like a lion cub. In fact, by that time visiting family friends and relations who had known him as a harmless little puppy were captivated by his beauty and at the same time strode past him with obvious trepidation just because of his size and, of course his growl. Yet as night progressed Shumba barked much less and together with Sheba slowed down and lay on their stomachs.

They sensed my movements with interest for a while before sleep completely claimed their consciousness, one after the other. Then soon after, I would retire on one of my favourite patches and steal some uneasy sleep. Thankfully, even to this day, I tend to surrender myself to deep sleep in just after the break of dawn to early morning and with some snatches here and there during the course of the day. The wide trunk of the huge old jacaranda tree in our garden served as part of the wall protecting the section of our yard behind our workers' cabin. The builders were reluctant to cut the tree and stump out the thick roots buttressing it firmly to the ground.

The management of the company building our wall had underestimated the ingenuity and skills of experienced thieves to reach targets and decided to leave it untouched. Moreover, by the time the builders came to that part of the wall new orders needing the company's attention were piling from other customers. They were now less than a hundred yards to join our border with the homestead of Whisky and family.

I chased away quite a few thieves intending to help themselves to mum's chickens. One thick branch of the same jacaranda tree was used by thieves to swing from outside into our yard using a strong rope. When they had not heard any barking for a while, they stealthily got the rope up.

One time I startled the thieves getting ready to sail into our yard. They abandoned the rope and left it dangling down a branch in their haste to flee. The workers always reported the nocturnal episodes to the family. As for our jacaranda tree, in the end, the nuisance branches were all chopped off. We liked to think that the act now deterred thieves because it was too risky for them to enter our homestead. After that, there were no more attempts to steal from our homestead. Two years later, two blocks from our property, a whole chicken run with fifty broilers ready for slaughter disappeared. It remained a mystery how the operation was managed because every security measure to prevent access to the chicken run had been put in place at that property.

I never stopped contemplating how to surmount the wall barrier closing us in. I wouldn't say I felt exactly claustrophobic but being confined took some getting used to. Really I should not have felt closed in because the yard was the size of a normal football ground, well almost, and there was a lot of room for us dogs to run about.

This is another trait we shared with our masters. If you were hooked on a certain habit there were all sorts of ways to justify the inclination, however undesirable. In those youthful days, I cherished those moments when I was free away from my usual home grounds. I knew it displeased mum and dad but despite my desire to make them happy the thrill I experienced out there in those brief moments was just too irresistible. I dreamt of all sorts of incidents, were it not for the wall getting in the way. One time in a dream, I smelt a human intruder outside the main gate.

I made for the gate but the spikes spelt danger. So I decided against it. I turned and ran down the driveway then turned round and entered mum's fruit garden. For the first time I realised the spikes were all round the wall.

The rockery had not been constructed yet. Fast as lightning, still in my dream, I made for the wall. After galloping several yards, I took off into the air and could not believe it when I found myself outside the gate on the ground! Suddenly I woke up and was disappointed to realise it was just a dream. I was still very much grounded, having made no attempt to jump at all.

Of course the wall is too high for me to jump. I reasoned with myself. I was not even anywhere near the wall. I had snoozed just by my kennel after my meal. Shumba was lying awake under the big bougainvillea and Sheba was at the water receptacle lapping the water up thirstily. All of us were behind the family kitchen a long way from the main gate and all sides of the erected wall. Suddenly I, thought, "Is it...the wall, is it that insurmountable?"

Chapter Eleven

The Offending Youth

During one weekend-break, in the mid-afternoon, Kate decided to go to the shops for some goodies. She took me on the lead to accompany her. She told me repeatedly she had missed me so much while cloistered at the boarding school.

"Come, let's go and buy some goodies," she said as she clipped the lead and patted me tenderly. After a few minutes of walking out of our main gate and down the road, we turned a corner onto a worn footpath and the block of shops came to view. Kate noticed a small crowd milling about the shops for choice items. She tagged at me to stop as we both registered a bus stationed by the petrol station with a few tired looking mothers inside the bus, breast feeding their babies and one or two toddlers playing around their mothers. A few elderly passengers also sat languidly on the bus waiting for the journey to resume.

We had to tread with caution as sometimes pick pockets had been caught red-handed plying their trade in such places. We stationed ourselves about thirty yards from the first shop, a supermarket. We were too nervous to go any further. I had no idea what was going on in Kate's head. As a child she was not allowed to enter the shop with me, a dog, in tow. She held the lead firmly in her hands. As for me I kept my cool trying to figure out what was going on.

I am hardly at my best with my neck in a lead and worse still with strangers milling around. Show me a dog, in the whole world, that finds the idea of a lead or leach exciting! On the other hand, Kate could not leave me tethered to a pole outside the supermarket with all those people from the rural bus bustling about the front grounds of the shops. She might have been trying to think which option was the best to take as we both stood out there with her left hand clutching her purse.

My eyes wandered towards the many passengers mingling with other customers both in and outside of the shops. It was all an exciting change in a day's routine. I was on maximum alert, throbbing with anticipation. The bus which plied between Harare and a particular province of the country had been known to divert and stop at this shopping centre on most of its long-haul trips.

The reason for the diversion was to afford passengers the opportunity to top up groceries to share with family members at their rural homes or pick some snacks to munch at leisure on the way. Then I saw something that sent my heart beating faster than ever before. He was an ordinary looking youth about seventeen years old clad in a faded blue t-shirt and a pair of dirty looking white jeans. His shifty eyes often flicked with interest at Kate's purse. I averted my eyes, looked elsewhere but edged to the left watching the guy sideways. Kate turned to pat me as she nervously ordered me to stay still.

"Don't move, Shungu. Keep still now," she ordered as she patted me anxiously.

Cautious not to meet Kate's eyes, the youth continued to behave suspiciously. Looking elsewhere but edging to the left, his eyes squinted anxiously at his target, the purse, pleased with Kate's weak grip on it. This guy had not reckoned with the guile of some guard dogs.

His body language convinced me he did not think I was worth any consideration at all in his grand scheme. He had missed the point and continued to ignore me completely. Even as he positioned himself for the deadly move, his shifty eyes still avoiding direct contact, he didn't notice me.

Here though, I have to explain something of relevance. Kate was born visually impaired so she had not noticed the thief with the same clarity as I had. I had noticed her visual deficiency at the house a few years ago, when she was approaching the fowl run to feed the chickens one afternoon. Unlike every other member of the family, she was unable to spot the door from afar. She turned her head this way and that moving with great caution. Then all of a sudden she smiled and advanced into the rabbits' section.

On sensing her mistake, she felt her way out and soon got to the right place. With an even wider smile now, she summoned the chickens, "Ku, ku, ku," and scattered the grain for the birds as they noisily waddled towards her to feed. After several similar observations, I came to the watchdog conclusion that she could be taken advantage of by bad people and that she needed protection. I was going to do just that now, to see that she was safe. The youth advanced toward his target.

As soon as he grabbed the purse, I nipped his right leg through his jeans without a single bark. He attempted to run but people blocked his way and one male from the shouting crowd retrieved the purse and handed it back to screaming Kate. That is when I started to really bark though still firmly secured on the lead.

A worker from one of the houses on the same road as ours who had come to the shops to buy something, ran to our house and called to the gardener, who turned out to be off and not home. Mum, who was reading the newspaper in the veranda walked towards the gate. As soon as she got the message she strode back into the house and assembled my medical papers then drove to where we were waiting at the shop.

Kate still held me firmly on the lead as she leaned against the wild tree at the entrance to the shopping precinct. The bus had left without the pick-pocket by now. A member of the Neighbourhood Watch who happened to be around had rendered the youth captive and sat him on the pavement.

The people had cleared when mum appeared. I could tell she was not happy with what Kate had done based on the strong warning she had given her. I could not mistake that look of subdued anger. I had witnessed it before when she was evidently unhappy about something unacceptable that any member of the family had done.

The first thing mum did was to look at the thief's bite, while reminding Kate that she was not supposed to come to the shops alone with me. Then she said, "At least the bite doesn't seem to be too deep. I feared worse. Since the incident happened outside our home we bear some responsibility, though the dog was on a lead. I'm going to take you to casualty," she said turning to look the youth in the face.

Then becoming more serious she asked, "Do you know you can be locked up for this: pick-pocketing? It's an offence, you know. Why did you do it? Still we have to follow the legal procedure," she mumbled the last words more to herself than to the offender.

The Neighbourhood Watch member would not let mum take the juvenile to the hospital alone. So he insisted that he accompany them instead of going to town as he had originally planned. Mum dropped us, then returned to pick the Watch man and the youth.

The doctor confirmed the bite was going to heal soon after treatment. "Mrs Mabvira, let me look at Shungu's medical certificates. Has Shungu been vaccinated against rabies? Oh here we are! You did well to bring this important document, the vaccination certificate. The dog is safe," the doctor said after a deep sigh of relief.

"Do you wish to sue…?" "No, I just hope the young man has learnt his lesson and will not repeat this foolishness," mum answered as the doctor scribbled a prescription.

"My daughter was born with a visual defect and I guess she just felt secure going to the shops with the guard dog. She is a spirited girl…"

"Never mind Mrs Mabvira, girls will be girls," started the doctor. Mum would not be interrupted, "…but has been warned not to walk the dog on her own.

However, I give her credit for retaining the lead firmly in her hand. In the heat of anger who could tell what acts of terror Shungu would have committed if unrestrained," Mum remarked as she took the prescription from the tired looking doctor.

"Thank you doctor," she said. She bought the medication from the hospital pharmacy and the youth was duly treated by a male nurse who exuded an unusually professional flare. The young thief looked remorseful alright. Whether troubled by missing his bus or by being foiled in his attempt to grab the purse true contrition would remain his eternal secret.

Mum gave him bus fare to enable him to get to his original destination the following day. Dad was livid when he heard what had happened in his absence. He soon regained his composure and together with mum had a good discussion with Kate. As usual when I met dad at the gate he had asked me what I was up to with a broad trusting smile. He patted me and then addressed Sheba and Shumba who had trotted to greet him as well before he took the driver's seat and drove his car down to the garage. He had been playing golf at the local golf course where by then; he had been a member for years.

We trotted close behind his car and ran past towards the backyard as he parked the car in the garage. As far as I was concerned the afternoon had proceeded superbly. I could not have wished to execute my guard duties more honourably. I was warmed by a pervasive feeling of ecstasy because I had protected Kate's purse. In the late afternoon of the following day, mum and dad were having tea outside in the veranda. I curled myself on the ground a respectful distance from them. I think Shumba and Sheba were enjoying the cool of the mango tree in the backyard as they often liked to do.

Well, from where I lay, my ears pricked up and watching mum and dad's expressions, I liked what I saw. The two were having what seemed to be a very lively conversation. Their faces and gestures when they looked at me conveyed plain happiness with me. I could tell at one point they were talking about me and my unique style of duty. I must confess I couldn't be more proud of myself. Predictably, with gleaming smiles they invited me to come nearer and we started interacting as we did as part of our quality time-some patting here, rumpling there and the rest of our little games. Before I knew it, it was over.

There was no point in my being jealous when dad invited

Shumba and Sheba who had suddenly shown up yawning from an afternoon snooze. Shumba had been trained to resist hurling his great bulk when greeting or interacting with any member of the family. But sometimes in his enthusiasm he would forget, prompting the family member concerned to immediately shun him.

Yes, all of us animal members of the family pack are not so reserved in displaying our craving for affection and the human touch. I had always suspected that most house pets were more indulged (with quite a few being downright spoilt rotten) than the outside working dogs. In a begrudging way, I envied them and all the undeserved fondling they got and if the bare truth be told, I did not actually regard them with that much respect. I thought they were sissy, to say the least.

However, the little voice of experience inside me now no longer agreed with that notion of mine. Or else why would millions of people-young, old, the elderly living on their own, people with disabilities and in particular the blind, enjoy the companionship of domestic live-in dogs and a variety of other pets. Not just as house pets but for some humans, as friends. Some dogs offered invaluable support to families and individuals in times of bereavement, while others played a major role in detecting criminals as well as containment of diseases. It is an undeniable fact that dogs have taken a giant leap into the rarefied spheres of medical and forensic science. Who knows into what other areas of life, dogs will venture and shine in for that matter? The sky was the limit!

Chapter Twelve

Shumba Enters the Agricultural Show

Shumba's greatest day came when he was driven to the annual Zimbabwe Agricultural Show. The previous day we had all been bundled up at the back of the truck with Sean, now 19years old, driving. At first we thought we were going to the Botanic Gardens and we got excited as usual, but then the gardener took a seat beside Sean. Right then our rising anticipation was dampened because the gardener never came with us for these weekend leisure excursions as he was off at the weekends. Then I realised further that from the flow of activities today it could not be a weekend

It didn't take long for it to dawn on me that our destination was the place I dreaded most, the vet. But this time we were not lead to the dreary medical section with the smell of disinfectant and evidence of some serious medical paraphernalia. We passed the dipping trough. So we were heading for the GROOMING SECTION.

We were on time for our appointment and were attended to immediately. There were two groomers working at great speed. We were inspected all over including the gums and teeth, the ears, the nails and so on. The actual grooming then started over each part of the body ending with a massage and a good brushing of our fur. Shumba had extra attention as he was the one entered for the show. Sheba and I had come for the most that could be done as routine grooming. There were no fancy styles as those I saw on some very indulged in-house or personal pets, which made them look like anything but dogs!

The Zimbabwe Agricultural Show was an annual event held in August during school holidays. During that time the tropical rains were still several months away, after the cold season. The autumn season was setting in and the earth was blanketed in different shades of orange as leaves from all types of trees and grass carpeted unclaimed land and roadsides. The watered leafy suburbs surrounding the showground offered cool greenery which rose over the high walls bordering each property and matched the scenery of the vast showground village. The village itself was walled in with high security outlets for vehicles and pedestrians.

A variety of exotic shrubs and an explosion of all types of brilliant flowers were in evidence everywhere in the village. Gum trees, msasa, munhondo trees, and all sorts of traditional Zimbabwean trees reclaimed in the reforestation programmes of the country were in evidence rising everywhere. A large number of exhibitors manage to grow and maintain ornate patches of exquisite green lawns as enhancing background to exhibits. The overall event was organised at a grand international scale. The exhibits came from all over the world and, contrary to the name of the show, it was not confined to exhibits of agricultural machinery and products only. Exhibitors also showcased motor vehicles, super craft work, and all sorts of animals including different breeds of dogs.

The hundreds of numbered stands and stalls were superbly lined up along clean alleys for easy access. There were also stalls for endless types of food items including sweet and savoury African, Asian, Italian and English cuisine (with English fish and chips topping the list in popularity). Government departments and charities availed themselves of the opportunity to advance their awareness and advocacy programmes by displaying their logos and chatting to viewers. Whole families could be seen sauntering at leisure viewing exhibits whilst they enjoyed coned and cupped ice-cream of varying flavours. It was an occasion of exceptional excitement for locals and visitors from far and wide, as well as their children.

Local and international traders and other prospectors bustled about with throbbing anticipation to clinch deals of all sorts and, in the course of the week, quite a few are finalised. At the centre of the village spread a vast stadium with terraced benches for the public on three sides. A colossal canopy covered a large area of the forth side of the stadium. In the canopy sat important invited guests including the top political cadres of the ruling party from all provinces of Zimbabwe, ministers, international diplomats and their families and topping the hierarchy, the President of Zimbabwe and his family.

A lot of group events were staged in the stadium arena to rousing applause from the audience. Even after the guest speaker, normally a president of a friendly African or other nation, and the President's address, the programme of stadium events continued till quite late in the evenings. It was to this grand occasion that Shumba had been registered as a participant in a dog show.

The long expected day dawned and Sean, accompanied by Kate, drove Shumba to the showground the day after the grooming. Shumba was served his food early and thirstily lapped down his drink of water as usual. By now I had long reconciled myself to sharing the family attention from time to time with Shumba and Sheba and so I was not bothered.

Shumba was a picture of beauty with his full bulk and well brushed glistening fur. He gave a pleasant lion growl as he was led to the waiting van Sean had just reversed out of the garage. Of course, Sheba and I stood by panting and swaying our tails in anticipation. It was soon made clear; we were not included in the trip that day. As the van disappeared with a loud, heightened roar we turned to each other and consoled ourselves by jumping about and chasing each other.

The Proceedings at the Dog Show according to Sean

Contrary to our fears the car parking area at the showground was not difficult to find. It was vast enough to accommodate thousands of vans, lorries and sedans. Everything had been so well organised that it was clear where we had to take Shumba. Shumba had to be on a lead throughout the occasion. We trudged from the carpark all the way to the dog show patch, which was almost on the other side of the show village - quite a walk.

It was not much of a struggle leading Shumba on the way. In

fact, we were proud to note that Shumba was turning heads not only because of his muscular bulk, that quite a few people feared, but also his winning beauty. It was agreed between Kate and I that since I was the one who had entered Shumba for the dog show, I would be the one to come forward leading Shumba before the judges. By coming early, we had avoided the hustle and bustle known to unsettle some dogs.

After presenting the entry ticket everything was explained to me including the requirement to queue up with the dog in fifteen minutes' time. The dogs under the control of their owners put up a good show of behaviour and so there were no confrontations between them. The degree of dog control by its owner was one of the crucial criteria on which the dog-owner relationship and interaction were judged.

We were instructed to fall into file and walk around the show patch while the judges took note of the general health, behaviour and presentation of the dogs. To my surprise I found out that I was the only African contestant. I did not make much of it since I had always participated in different things and really derived pleasure in working with dogs.

Each dog was judged against the standard characteristics regarded as ideal for a particular dog type. In other words, instead of comparing the dogs against each other, the judges focused on how far the dog's development approximated the idealised version of its breed in body parts and attributes including for example overall balance, head shape, teeth length, bite and so on.

They also assessed the dog's psychological traits such as the sense of security and trust it gave. While the judges discussed the contestants' performance, a few other events were thrown in to pass the time. The viewers including the contestants cheered. Kate as usual enthusiastically took part in the egg and spoon race and did quite well, beating several contestants.

Then after a long and anxious wait, a loud announcement was made telling us that the results were ready. Shumba came second in the contest for Alsatians, his health and teeth receiving a special mention as being in excellent state by the announcing judge. Some colourful awards were given but I cannot remember exactly what prize Shumba got.

The family had not yet bought a camera even though we loved travelling. Kate bought an ice-cream cone on our way to the van for our drive back home. Shumba's was a double whammy which he gulped down in no time and, characteristically, he started eyeing mine and Kate's alternately.

"So there you are! That's what happened today," Sean ended the narrative on the day at the agricultural show.

"Good for you, Shumba," I congratulated Shumba, gently nuzzling him for a second or two.

I dare say Shumba stealing the spotlight even just for that day only left me a bit put off. Make no mistake about it, I tickled with brotherly pride in Shumba' success. But it was hard to stifle the green-eyed monster of jealousy raising its gruesome head in me.

But then I quickly remembered how cool and accepting he was while I received special acknowledgements for my guard dog feats, and how well he endured my dominant streak. So, I decided to celebrate this moment with him. Sheba came and joined us in prolonged frolicking, running about and performing other happy dog antics all over the yard.

It was lovely and pleasing that the gesture of goodwill on my part in no way collapsed the hierarchy of dominance. In fact, we had become more trusting, accepting and comfortable with each other to the extent that even Whisky, whom I had frightened off the last time she tried to play with Shumba and Sheba, was now also comfortable among us. She now visited more frequently and if she was not slumped peacefully across Sheba's side, she would be playing games with Shumba, pawing and nuzzling or fondly licking each other.

Chapter Thirteen

David's Luck

Icould not completely forget the thrill of trotting on my own without a lead and unaccompanied by any member of the human family. But each time I looked at the cruel spikes of the main gate I found them so daunting and that I would trek back to find something to distract me from the gripping wanderlust.

One day I remembered that dream in which I had a compelling need to fly over the six-foot high spiked wall landing on my feet outside our homestead. In the dream, I had taken off from a distance of approximately five feet and actually made it. From then on I had been practising, in my wakened state, without much success. I preferred two of Sean's games we used to play. In one, we ran in a zig-zag pattern avoiding stationary obstacles and in the other we jumped across a bar strung horizontally and at each successful jump, the bar was raised higher. But after a certain point I would lose interest and not jump. I did not care about any reward no matter what it was, till after some weeks after which the game seemed fresh again. That was where the idea came from, but now in place of the horizontal bar was the wall which I had to jump over.

At each attempt to scale the walls, gravity pulled me down before I got anywhere close to the top but I realised I was making progress. It was not as if I planned a regular practice schedule, but instead it all happened haphazardly. Each time I made a greater effort to jump higher, until one evening my front feet scratched the top of the wall and, to my absolute frustration, I bounded back on the inside of the wall, and not outside as I had meant to.

But then, I thought, there was no compelling reason for me to get outside…yet. So I went about my usual routine without much incident. My reputation as a good guard dog had spread even further than the neighbourhood and even across suburbs, as the crime wave was the main topic of discussion. Word had gone round and reached my family to the effect that most unwelcome intruders had more or less declared our home a no-go area. But some of those who had been regaled with details of my heroic antics as a guard dog preferred to regard me as a challenge and not a deterrent.

By this time mum's brother Kane had long left for a job as an administrative secretary at the industrial sites and was very happy there. He had raised school fees for his younger brother for a school term and provided food for his mother at his rural home. Another relation had been living with us for some six months up to the day the following incident occurred. He was mum's cousin, David, who had been employed at an Avondale supermarket three weeks after obtaining six O'level passes. He aspired to be a male nurse and so he was hoping to train as soon as he was accepted into nursing school. He was required to report for work very early each morning, before everyone else had left the house, and so could not benefit from a lift from either mum or dad who both left for their work place at something to eight. A key was cut for him to use the backyard wicket gate which opened to Kirkshire Avenue. Several houses along that road had experienced attempted and successful break-ins and burglaries.

One home was targeted twice within the year till the owners had to employ professional guards from a reliable security company. I had a habit of lingering around the area near the wicket gate about the time David came home. By this time the main wall around mum and dad's property had been completed but the barbed wire fence had not yet been rolled over and secured along the wall. That had been the plan. One afternoon not long after I got to the backyard area, David came into view, hands in his pockets, whistling along. As he approached the gate he stopped whistling, took out both arms from his pockets and fumbled for the key in his jacket. I spotted two young men making for him. I suddenly remembered the gate was locked and took a few steps back before barking as I feared David would run back into the arms of the thieves. Within a minute, I had flown over the wall with such ferocity that I took one of the bad guys down to the ground with me, landing next to where David had been consigned by a dynamic blow from of the other.

The boxer had started rummaging David's pockets for money but soon gave it up to flee on witnessing the violent impact of my whole body on his mate. I was dazed for a moment then managed to scratch and graze the robber's leg as he started his escape. He scrambled to his feet and bolted in the wake of his friend. By the time mum and dad got to the gate to find out what was happening it was all over. I was still recovering from the impact of the jump and so had been unable to go after the thieves preferring to assert my authority by barking as fiercely as I could. David pulled out the key and limped to the gate where mum and dad waited burning with curiosity to know what had happened.

The story was so incredible that if mum and dad had not come to the wicket gate and found it locked they would have been left no alternative but to think David forgot to lock the gate. It would have been hard to convince them that David remembered to lock it as he rushed for work in the morning. "Are you sure you're alright?" mum asked David.

"I don't even know where those guys came from. Just as I sensed there was someone behind me I felt the blow and I was rolling on the floor when I realised there was more than one attacker. The next thing Shungu threw himself on the other bad guy before he joined his mate searching me for money. He ordered me, 'Give me all the money now! Where is it?!' I pretended not to know what he was talking about but then he fled as soon as Shungu was on his friend. I think Shungu bit him because he howled, "Ouch!! Maihwe!!" He scrambled on all fours at first then pulled himself up and, fast as lightening, followed his friend." David breathlessly narrated the incident to gape mouthed mum while dad shook his head in utter disbelief.

As soon as they were certain David was not harmed and his wages were safely tucked in his socks they fell on me.

"Shungu, how in goodness name did you jump over this high wall?" dad asked as he crouched to stroke my back.

It was more of an expression of wonder than a question to which an answer was required to be honest. Mum remained speechless with surprise at my breath-taking performance.

"Shungu, good! Good! Imagine what could have happened if you hadn't…Oh my God! Come!" Mum knelt and looked me in the eyes patting my face with both arms.

"Good boy, Shungu," she praised me.

I felt elated, really thrilled. I could see I had made mum and dad happy and that was just amazing. David was on cloud nine; I saved his wages for the whole month. He was well aware that anything could have happened to him if I had not routed the muggers before they had the chance.

"I could easily have been killed by those desperadoes. How did they guess I got paid this Saturday afternoon? They must have been watching me, studying my routine and I even suspect they have been stalking me from afar for some time."

"Do you really think they would go as far as that?" mum asked.

"Oh, yes, there is evidence of that. My fellow workers tell countless stories of handbag and brief cases snatching, with some victims sustaining grievous bodily harm or even death in the process. They say some of the victims have been stalked and their habits studied for some time before the muggers pounced on them," David told mum and dad.

The gardener, VaRoy came forth with stories of some spine-chilling incidents of muggings and robbery which had taken place in many suburbs before and after we moved to the current address. One of the victims had been given a lot of cash by a sister-in-law to buy some clothes for her new-born baby. The purse bulging with cash was grabbed with the handbag approximately fifty yards from where she had been handed the money. The young mother had been punched in the abdomen and left rolling on the ground, crying helplessly from raw pain. She hadn't completely recovered from giving birth. The cash was never recovered and the young mother refused to go out with her baby or even on her own for a long time after the incident.

Chapter Fourteen

The Botanic Gardens

On this Sunday afternoon, I knew we were driving out, probably to the Botanic Gardens. I had seen Sean handling the three leads and inspecting them before he placed them on the front seat of the van. Then later in the afternoon towards 3pm, after a rest, dad drove the van out of the garage onto the main car park. Shumba, Sheba and I were ordered to jump into the back of the van where Sean was happy to join us. Dad sat behind the steering wheel with mum beside him.

As soon as the van parked at the gardens, Sean clipped the leads on to the collars and jumped down first. He led me away while mum and dad took charge of Sheba and Shumba respectively. That afternoon there were more dogs than we had encountered ever since our first visit to this breath-taking place. The garden covered a vast area with trees and shrubs of various types interspersed with locally and internationally sourced flowers. There were also rockeries and a sprinkle of ponds breaking the monotony of the stretches of manicured grass.

Owners lead their dogs through clusters of trees waving in the cool wind. Man and animal enjoyed the late afternoon breeze which was soothing after a day of intense heat. There were lots of other families without dogs, just enjoying the afternoon. Couples seemed to warm to each other and be drawn together which was not really surprising given the beauty of the surroundings. But of course, dogs had to be on leashes to be allowed in the public garden unless owners arrived very early on in the morning when the place was quiet.

Sean and I ran together further down into the garden, though I was still held back by the loathsome lead. We came to a secluded bare stretch of land and Sean suddenly dropped the lead. He sprinted in front of me and I galloped behind faster and faster barking with pleasure. After one round, Sean stopped and I started jumping about with excitement. But when Sean went on his knees and ordered

"Come!" I calmed down and fell into his waiting arms to play.

Then we saw Shumba and Sheba straining to join us with mum and dad struggling to restrain them as they chatted quietly. Sean clicked the lead back on my collar and left me with dad. He freed Shumba and gave him a good run in the same spot as I and then it was Sheba's turn.

I was already protesting vigorously tagging towards Sheba and Sean. Shumba sank into a crouching position with exhaustion, breathing rapidly with his tongue out, dribbling a tittle, in itself a captivating sight of creation. As Sheba was led back to where we waited I gave him such a growl of disapproval.

"Stop it Shungu, stop! You have had your turn!" mum commanded firmly.

It was a long walk back to the van but the striking view of the setting sun we faced gave mum and dad something to comment so much about whilst we animal folks frolicked and nuzzled up to each other as much as our tethered confines allowed. In all, another happy memorable afternoon for the family, particularly for the animal members!

Chapter Fifteen

The Disappearance

By 1994 an electric powered gate had been installed at the main entrance of our homestead. Along the same road of ten houses, two other properties had long gone automatic and joined the thousands of low density and to a lesser extent, high density suburb residents who took to the technology like wild fire as soon as adverts were out. Mum, Dad and Sean used a remote control to open the gate so they no longer had to come out of their cars to manually open the gate. The other advantage was that on identifying a driving visitor, the family members could stay inside the house and control the gate from there.

Furthermore, as soon as the opening gate hit the end of the grove it reversed automatically to close. But the flaws in the new system were quite disconcerting. For starters, the powering motors were strong targets for thieves who sold them on the black market for next to nothing. Sometimes, Sheba or Shumba took the opportunity to shoot out while the gate closed behind a visiting driver, either on their way out or into our homestead. Most of the time I opted to track behind the visiting car barking furiously, till either mum or dad told me to stop. Then, crouching and probing into my eyes as they patted my back, they ordered me to 'go-now, good boy.'

I savoured the sound of the last pronouncement as I galloped to catch up with Sheba or Shumba back at the closing gate. Our new exciting game was to dash out as the gate slowly ground open and get as far down the road and back into the yard before the gate closed. I also led this naughty, challenging game after the last car had left for town in the mornings. I witnessed occasions, rare though they might have been, when Shumba had not made it through the gate and was locked out. Sheba did not go as far down the road as we did. She would rather stray into the thicket at the side of the road and take the opportunity to sniff about or mark her territory the way her ancestors did.

She then joined Shumba and I as we tore back bearing back down the road to beat the closing gate. We then shared the thrill of achievement together in dog fashion. Shumba's bark, though much deeper than mine and Sheba's was not as prolonged and insistent. I gave a sharp, stronger and longer lasting bark that held effect. The whole yard of our homestead was so vast that when someone was indoors, it was not always possible to tell whilst around the house, not to mention inside it, whether a dog barking around the main gate was outside or inside the yard.

One evening dad arrived from his rural home around 9 o'clock in the evening and was shocked to find Shumba waiting outside. He let him in and drove down to the garage with Shumba trotting in front to get to his kennel. He had to make sure Shumba was in front as the dog might slip back out while the automatic gate ground to close. We all came out to welcome dad. By this time, I was so confident in my well-honed skill of scaling the high wall that if I decided to wander a bit and meet one or two friends along the road, it was no big deal for me to jump up, cling to the top of the wall then safely drop into our yard.

But Shumba was not aware of such happenings, and even if he had been he would not want to bother with the persistent practice that it demanded. It was not every time that all the dog members of our family pack would be present to see mum and dad off to work and the children to school or college in the mornings. Sometimes any of us would be caught up on the other side of the building complex and only afterwards we would realise that they had long gone. The mornings were always so hectic that was not always possible for the human family to pause and check if all three of us were inside the great wall.

Most of the time they drove straight from the double garage, pressing the remote control in time to make it through the main gate before it closed. Otherwise, they would then have to waste time waiting while it slowly ground open again. So as soon as the gate opened, the three of us shot outside for a run. That way there was always ample time for us to gallop after the car and be back inside before the gate closed shut. Then the unthinkable occurred with untold misery for the whole family pack. Mum and dad rarely returned home for lunch. To avoid the rush, they preferred to patronise the many quality restaurants popping everywhere in central Harare, one or two of which even served some of their favourite traditional cuisine.

One Friday they decided to drive home in one car for lunch. It was quite a distance from the town centre where mum and dad worked and lunch time was such a stressful rush hour. As expected we came to the parking area to meet them. By now the three of us dogs, could read their body language and we sensed that they were pressed for time. Dad was in the passenger seat.

He alighted from the car first and in a friendly voice said, "Hello, Shungu and Sheba. Sit."

As soon as we were acknowledged in greeting we returned to our pranks whilst mum and dad disappeared into the house through the inner garage door. At such times we were not fazed but took comfort in the knowledge that we were loved members of the family. It was only that mum and dad were pressed for time as they had one hour for lunch time. Ruth, the efficient cook, had placed the food at the table as soon she heard the garage door open.

She then took a long lunch break soon after mum and dad thanked her for the food. By that time, I had a feeling something was not right but could not quite place my finger on it. We did not speed after them when they drove back to town. But then just as we finished our lunch, VaRoy noticed that not only had Shumba's bowl been untouched, but that he was absent and actually nowhere to be seen.

He called out Shumba, and walked around the house calling but still Shumba didn't appear. Then it clicked to me that the unexplained feeling of uneasiness emanated from the fact that I had not seen Shumba for some time that day. Now that I started

thinking about it, I could not remember having had sight of him at all even in the early hours of dawn. Sheba started making whining sounds walking about. I led a search throughout the yard barking furiously with Sheba behind me, but made no attempt to get over the wall. Sheba soon calmed down but looked confused as we trotted back and waited miserably for mum and dad to come home.

We lay down in the homestead car park, but not for long. As if prompted, we sprang up at the same time and cantered toward the wicket gate peering out through the thin gaps between the gate iron bars. We sat there looking expectantly far down Kirkshire Avenue for quite a while willing Shumba to materialise with no effect. Disappointment washed over us and so back to the car park we went and resumed our anxious waiting. Sheba dosed off for a while. I could not keep still. I wondered what had happened to Shumba. I really missed him already and began to imagine I had spotted his deep-tan form emerging from behind a bush, only to realise it was all illusion. Heads turned at every crunching sound or tree leaves sighing to the breeze expecting to see Shumba stomping impatiently to reach us, his face aglow with happiness only to be greeted by the vast emptiness stretching to the backyard wall of the homestead.

"What is it? You look so shattered, VaRoy?" mum asked the gardener half-way out of the car as she arrived home from work in the evening.

"It's Shumba. He has not been seen since meal time. I have gone round the block calling his name but he is not responding."

"What?! Good heavens! Are you sure he's not within the walls somewhere?" wailed mum in desperation.

"No, Amai. I called and looked everywhere. Shumba usually responds quickly to his name" Mum flopped back in the car, reversed and zoomed on her way out to search a wider area.

It had worked in the past. Whenever any of us had strayed outside the gates then spotted either mum's or dad's car as they called our names, we dashed to the car with excitement, happy to see the family. It was lovely and reassuring to be followed and with a sense of pride and confidence trotted home behind the car. But if we had wandered much further off, on spotting us, mum would alight from the car as she called our names. She would then open the car door to let us in. And so mum saw no reason why it would not happen this time.

But that day no Shumba galloped excitedly to follow mum's car after she covered numerous roads, crescents, avenues and cul-de-sacs. She looked utterly heart-broken as she drove back and came to share her disappointment with us. That night we barked, wailed and moaned into the early hours of the morning.

Our friends and acquaintances in and beyond the neighbourhood shared in our grief, something that was hardwired in our genes. The other dogs recognised the mournful timbre in our voices and, in response, chimed in harmony with us to show some kind of support. Weeks went by which then melted into months and the awaited calls remained a distant tantalising prospect. Each family member found some comfort in revolving a kaleidoscope of pleasant memories of our experiences with beautiful, gentle Shumba.

I often dreamt of the three of us lost in vigorous antics and games. Sometimes in the dream we would be running breathlessly behind sprinting Sean in our garden which then morphed into the heavenly Botanic Gardens - a favourite antic of dreams, the morphing I mean. Dad and Sean had combed everywhere including the kennels for strays in Waterfalls, even going to the police, but had drawn a blank. They had left Shumba's description and our contact details with the kennel management in case he was brought there for refuge as a stray or lost dog.

What was puzzling every family member was why no one bothered to check the collar labels which showed the telephone number of the police station covering our area. Dad checked with the police as much as he could without becoming a veritable time-wasting nuisance. Several visits to the distant kennels continued to be frustrating.

To, mum and dad the three of us had each been precious in our own way. Shumba was not only impressive in size and endowed with eye-catching natural attributes, but he had become a constant in our lives and a good friend to Sheba and I. Shumba was also mighty strong, so strong that if he had wanted to, his robust haunches would have easily crushed and pinned me down while his strong teeth tore me to pieces in no time, just like Shumba the lion. But despite my bullying and domineering tendencies, he backed down, not because he feared me, but because he did not want to hurt me.

Chapter Sixteen

The Craze for Electric Gate Motors

There had been a few attempts to steal the electric gate motor which I had frustrated not long after the motor had been installed. The local and national newspapers reported sporadic incidents of automatic gate motors ripped out by expert thieves some of them within a few weeks of installation. Mum's friend in the next suburb was devastated after experiencing a double tragedy of theft the same night.

One would have thought the thieves would be content with the gate motor but unfortunately for the victim family, one of them decided to inspect the inside of a shed leaning beside the main house. Without hesitation, he flung open the rickety door, clicked on his small torch and could hardly believe his eyes when they fell on a borehole motor. From another pocket, he drew out a spanner and in a flash, he was lugging the disconnected compact motor towards his waiting friend and a battered Alfa Romeo.

I knew there was something valuable about the motor connected at the left end of the gliding gate because I had looked on when the main gate was installed. That morning dad had let the installing mechanic into the premises and after exchanging pleasantries with him, dad assured the mechanic he was safe with me and drove off to work. On my part I had ceased nipping every stranger who stooped to lift any object from the ground in the homestead premises.

I would like to think I had outgrown the instinctive reaction as it gradually dawned on me that the habit did nothing much to ingratiate me in the eyes of mum and dad. So I curled myself on the ground watching as the engineer laid the track, installed the spiky gate and attached the motor. I saw him smile as the gate jacked and glided smoothly along the grounded rails to open and on the reverse to close. Sheba and Shumba had started barking at the strange moving phenomenon.

We had not yet conceived our dangerous game of dashing out as the gate opened and in as it closed. That frolic was still in the future but not so far off. The road which led to our house cut a bend just by our main gate back to a busy avenue that cross-cut a busier main road that traverses several leafy suburbs both ways. The road leading to our home itself was quieter with sparse traffic consisting mainly of cars from the only ten homesteads along it and their pedestrian domestic employees.

Of course, from time to time, both the former and latter received visitors coming down the same road. To a large extent, domestic workers would much prefer to use the backyard alleys through the wicket gate where these existed, like at our homestead. One would be forgiven to query my heightened anxiety over the security of the automatic gate motor in view of the comparative calm and seclusion of our patch. But throughout my watchdog experiences with my family, much had happened to underline the need for constant vigilance, more so in these suburbs of greater affluence. And so I found myself drawn to the precincts of the main gate quite often just to hang around. Sometimes Sheba came with me. Both of us took some time to get over the muffled gliding of the opening and closing of the gate.

There was something soothing about the sonorous sound the gate made and so we would be captivated until it came to a sudden clanging stop. Then we would both nonchalantly observe the outside scenery and life through the bars. If there was nothing that caught our interest, we were likely to fall back to our usual little games together or go our separate ways to our individual habitual devices. This particular afternoon I was mooching about in the shrubs and colossal palm trees nearer to the main gate, as had become my habit of late.

The downpour that had dropped an atmosphere of dark gloom had abated, the gloom had lifted and all of a sudden it was light again. You could smell the refreshing, uplifting air of wet earth. The usual cricket sounds and bird song could be heard in full throttle.

At that point, I observed mum and Kate, in the middle of the orchard flitting from tree to tree. They were talking and laughing much more like close friends with love and respect for each other, rather than parent and child. They lingered by a kidney mango tree groaning heavily with fruit. They were reminiscing about Shumba, talking and laughing as they plucked a few very ripe mangoes, dropping them into a bowl that mum held. Mum's fond memories were Shumba locking eyes with her as she rumpled his fur to return his greeting and how Shumba ran to her in response to her calling voice. This was when Shumba had popped out to meet his friends in the neighbourhood. She placed her palm on the left side of her chest, almost on the verge of tears as she narrated how Shumba's face would then light up with happiness at the sight of mum.

She then recalled how Shumba would jilt his company and gallop at once to meet her and follow her home. In these moments mum's conscience gave in to a turmoil of guilt and regret. But the one thing she was absolutely sure of was that there was no way that she would have kept the dogs tethered on a tree all day or closed in somewhere in a dark room. With a shaky voice, she expressed her hope that Shumba had landed himself an experienced family who could love and protect him better than we might have done. Then from where I stood, approximately three yards from the main gate, I spotted a man through the bars, confidently striding towards the closed gate. Instantly I barked whilst at the same time watching his reactions.

He froze with fright for a few seconds. Then, in my view, he committed the cardinal error. Shaking with fear he advanced towards the gate and quickly picked a small parcel which had slipped from his hands to the ground, turned and scrambled up the usual tree on the side of the road for refuge. Inevitably the demons in me were aroused. That did it, because there had been no connecting him with any member of my human family.

Mum and Kate were still engrossed in their memories of Shumba and unaware of the goings on near the main gate. I was livid. I could see him peering at me which sent me ballistic and I flew into the air over the gate spikes landing clear on the damp surface. Mum dropped the mangoes instantly and had already started calling me as I scaled the wall.

Kate looked on in utter disbelief as she followed mum to the gate. Mum and Kate witnessed the jump and soon other dwellers of the homestead including the employees and Sheba were drawn towards the gate. I was now jumping up in futile attempts to bring down the thief from the well- worn tree branch on which he clung when mum came through the wicket gate at the side of the main gate and ordered me to "sit".

I knew straight away I had to forget about catching the intruder. VaRoy approached mum and explained there was a mistake. The stranger was his brother VaJohn from Murehwa, one of the provinces near the city of Harare, who had come to spend the weekend with him at the worker's cottage. I had sprung into action to protect the automatic gate motor having mistaken vaRoy's brother for one of those bad people.

In the watchdog business one had to be vigilant and act quickly or it could be too late. Needless to say, I was remorseful for sending a decent person up a tree that way but I could not exactly enunciate an apology to mum and VaRoy. I knew mum and even VaRoy were aware of the reason, I reacted so wildly. They knew from experience my intentions were noble – I just wanted to execute my duties as watchdog. When I thought about it, owners of watchdogs must have been caught in an uncomfortable double bind.

On the one hand, they wanted the dog to safeguard them and their property against theft and danger but on the other hand, if the dog hurt the robber in the process, it would all become embarrassing. What I didn't know was that all along mum and dad had not been quite convinced that I had jumped the property wall by the backyard wicket gate the day I saved David's hard earned wages from muggers. But today mum and Kate had seen me clear the wall spikes to land safely on the mud outside.

And that was the high point of the day especially for mum who could not wait to narrate the events of the afternoon as soon as dad got home and even before he had entered the house.

Mum seemed to thrill in having had an edge over dad as she was the one who had witnessed me fly over the wall.

"Really?" Dad asked with interest.

"Oh yes, darling it was something to see hey Kate?"

"So the barbed wire project has to be called off," Dad's response was a kill joy.

"Suspended, why should we…?" Mum's spirits were deflated but before she finished dad cut in.

"In fact we have to drop the whole idea for a long while."

"You're joking, right?" "No darling, it's not a joke. With Shungu jumping walls like that, he can be badly hurt."

"Hurt? Now, now what are you talking about? We agreed, didn't we?" Mum's face flashed with recall.

"Oh! I now see what you mean," Mum remembered the story of a mastiff which was hideously lacerated when its head was caught between two strands of taut barbed wire.

Attempts to dislodge its head from the knots of the wire had the opposite unintended result of entangling the dog's writhing body further, as well as causing ever deeper bleeding cuts. Lucky for the hapless creature, one of the guards set the dog free and rushed it to the nearest clinic before its condition became fatal. The dog was reported to have survived after a long period of treatment.

"No, I wouldn't want Shungu to suffer like that."

"The penny dropped," Dad teased, eyes squinting at mum.

"Now, now don't rub it in. After all I told you that story ages ago. I had clean forgotten about it, can you imagine?!" Mum chortled.

Then she mumbled, "Yes, the barbed wire plan has to be killed." She nodded for a second as if to convince herself. Then she stopped and looked dad in the face and spat out, "definitely," patting a smiling dad.

Chapter Seventeen

Starting the Day with a Bang

I had noticed that mum had developed a soft spot for Sheba, a curiously unusual extra warmth. For the life of me, I could not fathom the reason for mum's frequent unsolicited attention on her and for what?! Sheba had never amounted to much as a guard dog. To call a spade by its name and not a gilded fork, Sheba was given more to snoozing than running around the yard. But in the last three months she seemed to spend much more time than ever curled up with her eyes closed in blissful sleep jolting awake at the rising pitch of her own snoring.

In an instant, the snoring resumed. But lately Mum would out of the blue appear with some treats in her hand, throw one or two my way in such a way that I often missed them and while I trotted to retrieve them, she pointedly called Sheba's name as she almost placed the tablets in her mouth making sure Sheba did not miss any.

These treats were usually round and in all sorts of colours though mostly white, with a sprinkle of pink, yellow and green. Sheba gulped them with much gusto and an irritating air of importance, circled round the spot and dropped back to resume her rest.

A little later I was convinced Sheba's food helpings had also been increased at meal times and mum had now taken to feeding us herself, especially at weekends, with Sheba being favoured with a good variety of special feed boosted nutritionally. But soon one morning I noticed Sheba dragging her drooping belly and it was not long before I worked out the reasons for all these unusual developments. Sheba was expecting puppies and our veterinarian must have had a hand in shaping the course of current events concerning Sheba's present state of health.

As usual mum must have sought some advice from him probably on how best puppies should be cared for at birth, not forgetting the wellbeing of Sheba herself during and after delivery. I remembered with some excitement how Tessa had presented just before the arrival of her ill-fated puppies.

Forgetting that I had been castrated to reduce my aggression and wandering tendencies, I had deluded myself into thinking that the puppies were my progeny and was really looking forward to spending some time frisking about with them together with Tessa. But it was not to be. One Sunday morning, I pricked my ears in disbelief to much squealing and snorting coming from Sheba's kennel. Immediately I was transfixed as I took in the miraculous sight before me.

Sheba had done it all by herself. There were six of them - six blind, blinking puppies, vying for an adventitious place to make the most of prostrate and nonchalant Sheba's comforting warmth. The squealing, simpering puppies soon opened their eyes rooting eagerly towards Sheba's bulging nipples for a good helping of milk.

At this blind stage in their life, they followed their mum's scent, warmth and bodily vibrations. Sean and mum made Sheba and her puppies comfortable in the scullery leaving the main kitchen door open to the backyard in case the puppies wished to walk around or Sheba needed to pop out to relieve herself outside in accordance with her training when she herself was a puppy. The puppies thrived and were soon taken to the vet under the watchful eye of Sheba.

Sheba was spayed a few weeks after the birth of the puppies as, according to mum, she had experienced the joy of seeing her own puppies. Mum had not allowed Sheba to undergo the procedure when Shumba was castrated as a grown puppy. "Moreover," the vet assured, "spaying would make Sheba maintain and enjoy good health, among many other advantages to her and to the family."

Four puppies were eventually sold and the remaining two were named Tonga and Terry. The money was dropped into the pet cash box for dog expenses, mainly training treats, toys, colourful eating bowls and other things.

For an animal which was disenabled from fathering my own puppies, I had-had it all. First it was Tessa's puppies which were all sold just as Tessa began to relax, soon after I arrived to play the big dad. Shumba and Sheba were absolutely beautiful as puppies when they joined our family pack. Imagine what I felt when I started romping with them all over the yard nudging them when they were naughty. And now I had Tonga and Terry, Sheba's growing puppies that remained under my close care after Sheba died. Sometimes they were very naughty, especially Terry.

He showed signs of being stubborn. But Tonga was like her mother in most things. I felt good inside - seeing them grow. They both looked healthy, beautiful and were very active too.

Chapter Eighteen

Fact or Fiction: Shumba's Fate

It was now many years since I had become a member of the Mabvira family. I felt I had lived a considerably satisfactory life, the family looked after their dogs to the best of their ability, especially considering that they had next to no experience at all with dogs at my point of entry into the household. Whisky had been quiet for almost a year. I had done my best to raise Sheba's thriving puppies. I just hoped that they had not inherited the ailment that claimed Sheba's life.

I had enjoyed the company of fellow dogs both at home and in the neighbourhood, though I lost a good pack brother in Shumba, who I still missed terribly. There had been a few conspiracy theories put forward about Shumba's disappearance. Sean and his two sisters latched on to the one which involved a white settler farmer and his African farm hand. The story goes that as the two drove into town they saw Shumba shuffling about in the overgrown dry drains on the roadside near the neighbourhood shopping complex. The travellers bought some food items including several strands of biltong which they started to share with Shumba.

The farmer, it is rumoured, asked a passer-bye if he knew the owner of the dog. The latter after a few thoughtful moments shook his head and said he had never seen the dog before. The duo made back for their vehicle.

After a minute, conferring between themselves, the travellers soon lured Shumba to the jeep which was parked carelessly around a corner, strategically facing the direction of the farm. Someone had heard the farmer remark, 'Now there is a hell of a fine dog!' The farmer's left hand kept pulling down his khaki shorts which seemed too tight for his pot belly and thick thighs. By this time Shumba had been hooked on the biltong. He did not need much cajoling to heave on to the door of the jeep to make for the stick of biltong deftly thrown inside by the crafty farm hand. Immediately, the farm worker levered Shumba into the jeep where he started befriending him, patting and stroking him.

The witnesses watched, speechless at the event unfolding before their very eyes. One or two had seen the loitering dog long before the visitors from the country came onto the scene. The rumour detail that even before the labourer was quite seated, his boss had stepped on the accelerator to zoom toward the main road towards his farm.

The witnesses to the abduction of Shumba were believed to have been the locals such as some customers who patronised the shopping centre, cooks, and other domestic workers in the suburb who were not even aware the dog belonged to a family in the neighbourhood. The news of the abduction slowly made the rounds at social gatherings within the domestic staff community such as beer outlets, corners where draft games were played at lunch time and basically anywhere that small groups of locals convened to socialise.

However, the news reached our domestic workers only several years after Shumba's disappearance. What made the abduction story hold further was the absence of any sign of a dead dog along or pushed on to the roadside as a result of it having been crushed by a motor vehicle.

Motor crushed cats and dogs were a frequent sight all over Harare but Shumba had not been identified as having met with such a fate. Shumba's was surely a story of abduction implying he could still be running about alive somewhere. But where, was proving to be an unsolvable mystery.

What was more frustrating was that the abduction story offered no factual information whatsoever that could help find Shumba.

Particulars as the registration number of the farmer's jeep at least would have helped mum and dad to resume the search for Shumba. Mum and dad could only hope that the story had some element of truth in it on which to cling to for some form of closure: that he was alive and well somewhere.

Chapter Nineteen

Shungu's Final Days by Wendy

One of the many pastimes I enjoyed on weekends, when my husband, Daniel, with unconcealed enthusiasm would drive to the golf course to spend some time with his mates or to his business office to catch up with his work, was gardening. I threw myself into planting and weeding with a demonic zeal not far from that of a miner speculating for gold.

Sometimes I felt an impatient urge to expend an imagined accumulation of energy. Then with a pick I would dig a whole patch and prepare a few beds for cabbage, rape and other vegetables. Sometimes I drove to plant nurseries for shrub and flower seedlings in season to brighten the home grounds.

I found these pastimes hugely refreshing, uplifting and effectively therapeutic. After all, my late father had numerous master farmer trophies acquired over a long period of time alongside his cherished life-time career in the police force. On the whole, our experienced full-time gardener did an excellent job of it during the week considering, he had the whole vast homestead yard of shrubs, bushes and flower beds to manage. I was not fussy and so he had been assured and advised to spread his work over a long period and not overwork himself.

Sometimes I engaged part-timers to help with lawn manicure and other minor trimming tasks, including general tidying up of the yard which mostly proved worthwhile. But, sometimes, one could not help develop the impression that their work was rather slapdash and on occasion, slapdash to a disturbing degree. As part-timers, some of them felt it was to their economic advantage to fit in jobs with several home owners in a day in order to make more cash for their families. This tendency worked marvellously to the advantage of the part-timers themselves but not so much for the employers who would then be compelled to either ignore these tendencies or hire alternative labour.

All the while I weeded away, my dog pack would not be far from me. They would trot off to the other end of the homestead and loiter around the closed electric gate or some other part of the garden. But soon they would be heard galloping down back to greet me and play around where they could see me.

On this particular day, as I bent to do a bit more weeding, a familiar thundering sound made me turn and there they were trotting towards me, tongues out and tails wagging fast. By now they knew how to approach me as the "magic of my touch" and sweet-talking brightened their day, giving them joy beyond measure. On this Shungu's final day, as I knelt to greet him, Tonga and Terry, I could see we had come a long way from when they would have hurled their whole bodies on me in a savage excited greeting.

They now heeded the commands to "sit" or "stay" calmly, well almost, while I patted them saying "good boys." During these moments of quality exchange, I took the opportunity to examine their state of health and pick whatever creepy crawlies, I found ensconced on their bodies. I was pleased to note none of them had picked up the dreaded ticks and other undesirable insects since our recent visit to the vet for a dip. But I noted again how Shungu was showing signs of increasing age, particularly around the muzzle.

The fur coating around there was now completely white at seventeen years of age. His body remained mainly a glistening black, still robust and agile. He was amazingly masterly in his bearing, alert and energetic and above all, excellent as a watchdog. In all his life with us he had never been brought down by any illness of significance.

This was why the rasping dry dog cough which wrecked him several years ago remained such a dreadful, stressful memory with me to this day. I had never heard such a wrecking cough in all my life. It went on for weeks till I eventually had to take him to the vet. I was expecting the vet to come up with some damning pronouncement to describe Shungu's state of health from the disturbing way the cough sounded. The vet did not think the cough was serious enough to warrant antibiotics.

Much to my dissatisfaction at that time, the vet was convinced a prescription of pain killers would suffice to allay any pain or the discomfort that Shungu may have felt. What struck me about Shungu at that time – and, as a family, we have found it eternally quite amusing, was his enduring fear of the vet. Any family member who saw Shungu squirming before the vet was bound to wonder in disbelief, "Is that Shungu, the fearless dog?" The vet, on his part, had warned that the virus was often infectious and that left me jittery expecting the other thriving dogs to be brought down anytime. But soon the coughing miraculously ceased and the other dogs continued to romp about in good health.

Seeing Shungu striding across our yard made words like "majestic" and "fearless" come to mind. He was indeed fearless, powerful and self-contained with a quiet aura of superiority about him. Shungu's fear of vets was somewhat a leveller and all consuming, and often reduced him to a shivering wreck. He would literally tremble, twitch and whine in anticipation of the needle jab, real or imagined, with his now shaking tail down between his legs no matter how much we tried to reassure him by word and touch! He was only happy to jump into the back of the truck when it was all over and head back to his familiar patch in our yard. The fear lasted to the end of his life. I often felt I should have listened to the veterinarian's advice pertaining to the effect of pregnancy on the health of some dogs.

There was no way to know for certain whether Sheba's arthritis was inherited or came by as a result of her having puppies. But Sheba suffered much from this crippling disease which eventually resulted in complications from which she never recovered. She was a treasure for some eight years during which she added grace to our home. But now I realised that the death of an animal after a long ailment tended to prepare you for the inevitable.

And when it happens it becomes easier to cope with. However, looking back at what Sheba endured for almost five months, sudden death, though still undesirable, saved animals from prolonged suffering. Shumba disappeared from our home in the prime of his life. He had contributed immeasurably to the overall quality and general ambience of our home.

In his quiet way, he rendered great support to Shungu's rather aggressive approach as a guard dog. He was able to do this, not so much by his bark but sheer size and a definitive degree of subdued authority. A sense of guilt always sweeps over me at the memory of his disappearance. As time went by I learnt to expunge the uncomfortable feeling by recollecting the good times we enjoyed together, rumpling his fur not just for a reward, though which it was for that most of the time, but also in greeting and just in appreciation of having him around.

It was comforting to remember that at least I was not guilty of being ever so distant from him. In many ways we may not have been consistent but we made it a point to interact with our dogs as often as we could. I should also acknowledge that it was only possible to achieve the standards of dog care we maintained because of the help of our domestic team of a housekeeper and a gardener. Shumba did not succumb to illnesses either. I remember him in a head cone once after he sustained a gash at the site of his ribcage in a fight with a strange, vicious dog. Dan and I were walking Shumba on a lead.

The attacking dog was also on a lead but he lurched out of the control of his mum. Dan had to apply all his strength to rein in Shungu who went mad and was tagging to retaliate. Shumba had quite a few stitches, some tablets and the head cone to stop him from licking the wound and delaying its healing. I realised from research that there were just as many medical conditions and injuries that afflicted dogs as did humans, and like humans some of the conditions were inherited down the bloodline.

Nothing had prepared our household for the dramatic death of Shungu. As far as we were concerned Shungu still had a long life to live. On that particular day after lunch, we drove out for the weekend grocery shopping. Shungu, Tonga and Terry, now grown puppies, trotted behind the car up to the main gate. Dan had just asked for Shungu when he showed up majestic as ever, striding as if he was the very master of all he surveyed as poetic dad always mused.

The dogs stationed themselves at the gate rapidly whipping tails from side to side, eyes fixed on the disappearing car. Even before Sheba died, our dogs had long stopped lurching outside the yard as the electric main gate hummed open and close. I looked behind and there inside the gate, staring at the departing car, the pack stayed put. In the car, we talked briefly about those difficult times when the dogs would lurch out of the gate to follow any exiting vehicle as the gate slowly closed. Now we could laugh about it but at that time we were at a loss. It was lovely to think the trouble was all in the past.

"How did you do at golf this morning? Tell me did you achieve a birdie today?" I startled Dan who had been concentrating on his driving. He turned briefly to eye me with interest.

"Oh, not just once but a few times. What do you think I've been doing all these years? They say practice, practice, practice. But, of course, I don't aspire to be an Olympic champion. I just enjoy the game and I find much pleasure in keeping it that way," Dan answered breaming with excitement at the memory of success.

"Even then I don't know how anyone of you golfers manage to hit the little ball for such a long distance over tall trees and score into those little holes," I remarked slowly shaking my head in despair. "You gave up too soon," Dan observed.

"Who? Me? I thought that was a pure waste of time. Gardening seems to meet quite a few of my needs - recreation, the joy of seeing plants grow and, best of all, making it happen. My canine friends check on me from time to time, eh!" I said as Dan parked the car and we entered the supermarket.

On our return we sat outside in the veranda for a cool drink, chatting and laughing. As usual Shungu and company curled up a few yards from us. While the younger dogs dozed off for long periods, Shungu often raised his head to train his eyes on us. Today his gaze was thoughtful as if he had a premonition somehow that sometime soon he was going to dress us in gloom by his sudden death. At one point he sauntered quietly to Dan who patted him saying the key words of praise and appreciation, demonstrating his love for the pack. We gave all the dogs their bones starting with Shungu of course and then the fast growing puppies orphaned by Sheba a few years ago.

"Oh, my! Tonga and Terry are shooting up and so healthy! Now which one is which? Never mind. Hey, Shungu, you're doing a good job with the young ones. Come. I think he could have done well as a father if he was given the chance."

As he patted him, he remarked, "Darling, we have been really lucky with this guy." When evening came, we all went for a short ramble together with the dogs jumping around us within the walls of our yard.

"Who did all this work? I came this way this morning just before breakfast, all this wasn't there," Dan commented as he observed what I had accomplished in the vegetable garden that morning.

"Guess who?" I teased.

"Hey, you are your father's daughter indeed!"

"Absolutely," I said. "So shall we say master farmer, trophies are on the way?!"

"Not a blinking chance." We both laughed as we walked into the kitchen where we scraped something light for supper.

We had dropped the idea of dining out that evening as we enjoyed our home together. The dogs were quiet and out of sight, playing about or resting somewhere in some far-off part of the yard. Normally when we were in the garden, they would be mooching about around us hoping for some attention. In the evening, we were listening to music, mainly Oliver Mutukudzi, when we heard a decisive knock at the kitchen door.

"Who is it?" I shouted and Dan raised his hand to stop me from rushing to the door. He repeated the question as he, with some impatience, strode to the door.

"It's VaRoy's wife, Baba. Roy is not here." the gardener's wife had to raise her usually husky voice higher to be heard as she identified herself.

She then proceeded to announce, "Something must be seriously wrong with Shungu. He is lying on the path to our cottage struggling to breathe."

"What?" I bolted to the opened door. Dan had quickly assessed Shungu by the outside lamp lights and asked me to bring the key of the truck to the garage.

"It's bad," he said to me as he was already carrying him round the house to the garage.

I could tell from his quick strides and the way Shungu breathed that he was in a grave state.

Within seconds, Dan was reversing the car – fast! "You can't leave me behind; I'm coming with you. What's happened to Shungu?"

I demanded. "But I thought Shungu spent a good day. What could get bad so suddenly?" Dan mumbled as we sped to the veterinary surgery in silence. We found the surgery near the university grounds closed. But the surgery on Samora Machelle Road around Park Lane Hotel, another twenty minutes' drive away was open. It was Saturday evening and so we could not believe our luck when a man in uniform opened the door for us. The vet cast one glance at Shungu and sailed into a sizeable room asking questions in quick succession as the palm of his right hand indicated to Dan to place Shungu on the operation table in the middle of the room.

Within several minutes the veterinary assistant, as we came to know, had set the drip running. Our eyes were fixed on his every move. But with each passing moment, Shungu's breathing was getting tighter and more laboured.

"Why is he frothing at the mouth? What has happened to Shungu? He was alright all day!" I asked, my face strained with concern and taking a few steps towards Shungu.

Dan pulled me and held me close to him as we tried to take in what was happening before us. The vet continued to busy himself silently for a few more minutes before responding.

"Sometimes this condition can result from a snake bite, snake poison or a heart attack. Or, at 17years of life, most likely just the effect of ageing," he offered eventually. For a brief moment, my thoughts turned to guessing the vet's origins piqued by his strange accent.

He was so strongly tanned he could be described as dark with a Spanish accent and quite composed in manner. He was probably in his forties and heavily built.

"Oh, please, get him well for us. We don't want him to die. Oh Dan, Shungu is..."

"Darling, you can't say that. Let's wait and see. You can never quite tell with illnesses, better to keep positive, and hope for the best."

The vet then advised us to return home and get some rest. He promised to phone us as soon as he came up with a definite diagnosis.

"We will see how Shungu gets on now - is that alright? Let's see how he responds to the transfusion," he tried to reassure us.

He kept his voice very low and was avoiding much eye contact with us. At that point, Dan whispered into my ear, "I think we better go and let the vet do his work. Let's do as he suggested."

We both gave Shungu one good look, wondering whether it could be the last we saw him alive. It was 12:30am when the phone buzzed.

I strained for the receiver with dread and Dan leaned towards me to catch the message. I dropped the receiver with a scream but soon composed myself to break the news to Dan. He had already guessed. It was the news we had dreaded most. The vet was due off duty at 7:30am, by which time Shungu would have been incinerated.

"We would like to see him, please, before he disappears from our life for good," I pleaded with the vet.

"Well try to make it at half past six, understand?" There was no misunderstanding what was bound to happen if we delayed. In the morning, that sad morning, we took some flowers including a red rose from our garden, Shungu's dwelling grounds in life, and drove to the vet's surgery. Upon arrival, we were taken to where Shungu lay lifeless, cold and free from the gripping pain of the previous night. Sean took a glance and left the dog incineration parlour, grief-stricken to continue privately outside. Despite my husband's efforts to restrain me I braced myself to get nearer and give our cherished friend a calm respectable pat on the forehead.

"Bye Shungu and thank you," I said before stepping back and walking out to join Sean who was leaning by our car, his anguished face looking down and one arm akimbo.

My husband walked to the reception where the bill to cover the costs awaited us. As Dan strode to the car Sean got in and before his father settled to drive he shot out of the car, "Dad, just wait for me. It will take just a second."

Before Dan could say a word, Sean dashed back into the surgery and was back out just as fast. Dan and I suppressed the need to ask Sean the reason why he had gone back into the surgery, or maybe we decided to leave it for later. In the car ride back home Sean maintained a puzzled silence.

Then he moved, "I was not even around to soothe the pain a little. Maybe Shungu would still be alive and well right now." "Now, now, do not start blaming yourself." "But daddy he looked so well yesterday, no sign at all, not even a premonition. What happened to him, what did the vet say, Daddy?" Sean demanded. "The vet didn't seem so sure, but he muttered something about Shungu possibly having been poisoned or bitten by a poisonous snake or quite likely the effect of old age." I answered.

We drove in thoughtful silence for some distance. When Dan decided to respond his words were philosophical. He started by pointing out that there was no way the vet was able to arrive at a conclusive cause of Shungu's death without performing an autopsy on Shungu.

Then he explained that performing an autopsy on dogs was a rare service which only the very well off could afford.

"Anyway, all these enquiries would not bring Shungu back. It is all to no avail in my view."

"Oh, I don't know how I'm going to get through this. I miss Shungu already. Poor Shungu," I agonised.

Then Dan said, "I would advise that we take comfort in the good fortune we have had to own such a dog as exceptional as Shungu was for all these years.

You know how lucky we have been in that respect. I needn't say more," he reasoned.

"Yes, daddy you're right, but at the moment I'm still trying to get used to the idea of life without Shungu, poor Shungu." Sean said.

"I'll never forget Shungu, what a dog! What a treasure, gone!" I yearned. Both girls were studying overseas at different universities.

We had to decide the appropriate way and time to tell them the sad news. On Monday evening after work a beaming Sean came into the lounge where Dan and I sat.

He announced, "Mum they have given us Shungu's ashes for disposal. We will keep them till the girls return from abroad and undertake a little farewell to Shungu, scattering his ashes."

"What a brilliant idea," Dan and I said, our spirits lifting at the prospect. "But how did you manage that?" Dan asked.

"Oh well you remember before we drove back from the surgery yesterday I popped back to see the vet?" Sean reminded us.

"Of course we did not know you wanted to see the vet. We thought you had forgotten something inside." Dan answered.

"Well, I went to ask for the ashes before he disposed of them. He was so understanding and advised that I saw him Monday afternoon. And here we are!"

In a few months, we were to be with the girls in England for Thembi's graduation. But to avoid possible catty accusations about delaying to tell them about Shungu's death, we decided to let them know about it while they visited with my cousin in an English county the following weekend. We were together with Sean when we phoned the aunty and the girls. Just like we feared they were shattered.

But the mood dramatically changed to cheer at the news that we had Shungu's ashes with us at home in a container in the family library. "When we come back home after the graduation we shall scatter them together. Each one of us must think of the places Shungu liked best within the grounds of our home here," I said. Happy that the girls had handled the bad news better than we had feared, Sean went into further details expressing regret he was not home when Shungu fell ill.

"Anyway, see you when you come home. Only mum and daddy are coming for the graduation. Here is daddy," Sean said as he handed the receiver to daddy who needed to discuss the preparations for the graduation in England with Thembi.

Sean sounded more cheerful after sharing the sad news with his sisters. The first Saturday of our return from England had been set aside as Shungu's day. It was a sunny mid-morning with a refreshing cool breeze lightly blowing the tree leaves above. That suited us marvellously because today's occasion was going to keep us outside for almost an hour. It was just the family, the five of us.

The workers had their own weekend arrangements and weren't back on duty until Monday morning. Shungu's ashes were scattered with a small shovel in three places, his favourite haunts. The atmosphere was more celebratory than sombre. There were lots of memories to go back on. The day went well.

"That was very thoughtful of you mum and daddy to wait till we could scatter the ashes together," said Kate getting all emotional.

"Yes, daddy," echoed Thembi catching up with me, and putting her arm on my shoulders whilst looking me in the face, she added, "and you my mummy."

"We miss the dogs so much and Shungu's charm and bossiness, hey." "No. Thank Sean, for that. He's the one who thought of the idea," said Dan.

Yes, though the family continued with the daily routine as if nothing had happened, every now and again sadness would descend upon us at the memory of Shungu's death, especially in the first days, and probably weeks. The personal sense of security of the family as a result of Shungu's watchdog performances had been shaken so much at his passing. We started locking and bolting doors and windows assiduously at night, to a degree we had never contemplated before when Shungu and Shumba were around.

Daniel had a business in his home village 500 kilometres from Harare which needed attending to from time to time. As I held down a full time professional job, I was only able to accompany him during weekends and, even then, not on every one of those trips. But quite often he was needed there during weekdays as well. Even when I had relations in the house I was assailed by all sorts of fears of what nightfall might bring.

The confidence, the complete sense of security I had enjoyed over the years had gone. So how could I not miss Shungu? It was not like I ever thought or imagined I would feel. Indeed, as we soon learnt, the reputation he had built for himself in life extended for a period long after his demise. Gradually a lasting sense of security descended upon the family. Terry and Tonga grew up to be big in stature but the two of them together were not as energetic, colourful or feisty as Shungu.

Of course, dogs are almost as individual as humans with their own peculiar characteristics. Dan and I were grateful that with Shungu's death there was closure. We had the opportunity to run around and do everything in our power to save his life. We were also able to scatter his ashes.

What more could we wish for? As for the unfinished business, the barbed wire topping of the asbestos wall for added security was completed around our property in 1998. The work had been put off years earlier to protect Shungu from injury when he jumped over it. Terry and Tonga were not as forward and inclined to jump over six foot walls as Shungu was. My life's journey with dogs in our family has been far more enriching in ways I could never have thought possible before I welcomed them into our home.

I remember as a teenager giggling in ridicule at the degree of intimacy some people shared with their dogs especially those from the western world. Even much later in my life as a working adult it was beyond my comprehension the way owners stressed to distraction over the death of a dog, especially white owners. Even as an adult I was still not all that convinced till Shungu came into my life.

Gradually, I realised that to make the most of the shared life with dogs, owners had to be prepared to afford their dogs much more than food. Would-be dog owners had to be prepared to give a lot of thought as to whether they had the disposition to offer a dog a reasonably comfortable life in their homes. Apparently, there have been a lot of studies on general dog care, dog health and other aspects of dog life, including books by individuals who, like me, have owned dogs. I found the information extremely helpful in my attempts to broadly understand the behaviour of dogs. Shungu has featured in a number of my dreams and Shumba to a lesser extent.

In the last one, I had been gripped by an anxiety very much akin to a premonition. In broad day-light an angry stranger was sprinting down the driveway as I walked past the car park heading for the orchard. I noticed that the intruder had a gruesome looking weapon which he started brandishing as he advanced to plunge it in me.

Next thing I knew Shungu flew from under the bush near the willow trees baring his teeth and bringing the killer down before he hurt me. I was unaware that I was screaming in reality when Dan shook me awake calling out my name,

"Wendy!"

"Shungu!!! I've just had a terrible nightmare. There was an intruder and Shungu appeared from nowhere to save me. It was horrendous, oh! I'm sorry to wake you up," I apologised trying to pull myself together and resume sleep.

But I couldn't.

It was Dan who pulled me to him and his bass voice groggy with sleep, mumbled, "Not to worry, Wendy. It's alright. Come let's try and get some sleep now, shall we?"

Chapter Twenty

Epilogue: Second Generation

TROY Kate 's family dog

Kate is the older one of my two daughters. Her family's dog today is a lovely Staffordshire bull-terrier. Contrary to the rushed manner in which Shungu had come into our Mabvira family long ago in 1980, a series of events over time led to Troy being welcome into Kate and her husband's home. It so happened that one late afternoon, Kate's husband-Edward and their two girls met and chatted with owners of the dogs, pregnant Roxy and Diesel, in the local park. This happened a few times before Troy and his five siblings were born. Kate's family were not even thinking of having a dog in their home. The dog owners notified Kate's family about the birth of the puppies. On the first visit to see the new-borns, they were captivated by one of the feisty ones who had pushed his way through his siblings to clump his toothless mouth on his mother's swollen breast for a hard swig of the milk. The dog owners encouraged my daughter's family to visit whenever they wished to spend some time with the puppies.

During one of these periodic visits the cheeky little one snuggled in Kate's lap and when Kate, enthralled, playfully lifted it high she noticed the puppy reminded her of another dog. The puppies had black slick fur with a number of white patches on other parts of the body. But the visiting family's favourite puppy sported a distinctive huge patch spreading from his neck towards the chest and then it clicked!

The blind squealing, wriggling puppy bore a striking resemblance

to Shungu. He kept waddling and rolling between them and its dog mum. By this time the visiting family had irrevocably fallen in love with the white chested puppy and even before they took him home they had started to research a bit on dog care.

The children, Sarah and Chloe, insistently begged the parents to take the puppy home, but the parents kept silent on their intentions till the afternoon they celebrated the seventh birthday of the first born Sarah. As grandmother, I attended the event as well. The surprise presentation of the puppy to Sarah was the high point of the day for everyone, except me. The reason was that I harboured reservations based on my anxieties that at some point the dog might savage and hurt the children badly. The younger girl was aged just 3years then.

There had been media coverage of live-in dogs assaulting young and old members of families in Great Britain. My heart reached out with great sorrow to the families who had experienced this misfortune, something that could happen in any household.

The puppy was named Troy. The first few months of living with the puppy were quite difficult. The family found it increasingly difficult to cope with the demands of keeping a domestic pet in a flat even with 3 bedrooms like theirs. But they had no regrets. There was no going back from the current happy position they were in.

Warmth alone was not enough for puppy-Troy, who found it difficult to fall asleep. Just like human infants, he needed to know a family member was with him. His acute sense of smell would tell him whenever the tending family member had withdrawn from him. He would then moan and whine persistently making it difficult for the family to sleep and disturbing the neighbours into the late hours of the night. Kate and Edward remained positive that things would get better with time. Sarah and Chloe played and to this day, still play a major role in caring for Troy who both girls adore.

Toileting was another challenge that the family had to deal with. They got around it by taking him out to the park for walks with black bags as many times as the other demands in the life of a modern family would allow.

The best time for Troy was after school when the family played all sorts of games with him, and him biting into the toys they had bought for him. They also walked Troy in the local park on the lead under adult supervision. On a few occasions Troy and some of his siblings housed in the neighbourhood would bump into each other there in the park. There followed a big celebration as the dogs noisily greeted each other tugging both parents by the leads to get closer and nuzzle as friendly dogs do. The new owners took the opportunity to socialise together at these encounters. They would also take the opportunity to update each other on how they were adjusting with their pets, sharing valuable information on dog care.

Kate's children knew from a very early stage that Troy loved to play and that though he might appear to have an aggressive approach, he was only inviting them to have some fun with him. The children always responded accordingly with stroking, patting and rubbing his back for several minutes, then ordering him to "stop," then pointing "catch" before rewarding him with a cuddle for being a "good boy." It was not as easy as it sounded to train him, but I noticed during my visits that the family was coping very well.

Troy looked healthy, happy and confident. Troy is as manipulative as Shungu was. He is quick at working efficient ways of achieving or getting what he wants.

For example, Troy has been trained to lie down on his rag in a certain part of the lounge after greeting visitors coming into the house. Whenever I visit he comes to me for some extra stroking, something he is forbidden to do with any visitor. He demonstrates a high level of thinking rarely associated with dogs' brains.

As soon as he hears Kate's voice in the kitchen, he will turn back to his rag in the lounge and pretend he had never moved. For behaving so well he is showered with the desired compliments and a brief interactive play. Both Edward and Kate offer Troy quality time especially when he greets them when they get in home from work.

He is also forbidden to lie on the sofa but sometimes, after everyone has fallen asleep upstairs he descends the stairs to curl up quietly on the sofa in the lounge. If he hears a door opening upstairs, he dashes up the stairs towards the rag on the landing. But he no longer tries to rip up the leather upholstery of the sofas as before.

Troy is given a soapy wash periodically, towelled dry and brushed to prevent infestation with creepy crawlies and bad bodily odour. He is taken to the same veterinary surgery with one or two of his neighbouring siblings. He thrives on a balanced diet of home cooked food and water including carefully monitored treats to prevent weight gain.

Final Remarks

As a grandmother, it is gratifying to know that my grandchildren already practise dog care and dog health principles. They have no doubt had a head start in the practicalities of living with dogs which I did not have when I started with Shungu! All dogs are animals liable to be confused and run amok sometime.

I want to think it might help to consult with dog specialists, where possible, when considering to live with a dog. On the whole with the right management dogs can bring immense joy in the family. Ivy Hove

Bibliography

1: Clunes, Martin. A Dog's Life, 2008

2: Dalby, Liz. Happy Dog, 2007

3: Farthing, Pen. One Dog at a Time, 2010

4: Flint, Elsa and Meadows, Graham.

The Dog Owner's Handbook, 2001

5: Fogle, Bruce Dr. The New Encyclopaedia of The Dog, 2000

6: Gunliffe, Juliette. Showing Dogs: The Exhibitions' Guide, 2007

7: Hall, Derek. The Ultimate Guide to Dog Breeds, 2016

8: Hare, Brian and Woods, Vanessa. The Genius of Dogs, 2013

9: Larkin, Peter Dr. Complete Dog Care, 2003

10: Martitz, Nico. Your Sick Dog, 2004

11: Romp, Julia. A Friend Like Ben, 2011